SARTAYA

Donald F. McGee

Loconeal Publishing
Loconeal Select
Amherst, OH

SARTAYA

Cover Design Concept by Brian McGee

Edited by Kathy Watness

Published by Loconeal Select. Loconeal Select books can be ordered through booksellers, Handcar Press Distribution or by contacting:
www.loconeal.com
216-772-8380

First edition: 2014

ISBN 978-1-940466-11-8 (Trade Paperback)

Printed in the United States of America

ACKNOWLEDGEMENTS

I am grateful for the patience of my wife and partner in life, Karen, and her encouraging words that helped me to write my first fictional novel—Sartaya. I am also very thankful to my sister Lynne and my Mom Helen, who has since passed, for their gracious time in proofreading the earlier versions of this manuscript and offering their constructive criticism. I really appreciate my talented son, Brian, for his wonderful artwork and suggestion of a Wolf's Paw for the book cover. It was perfect for this story. Last but not least, the professional services provided by Handcar Press and Loconeal Publishing Group have proven to be an invaluable resource in this whole effort.

DEDICATION

To the "First People" who migrated to and hunted in the virgin forests of North America 6,100 years ago. These adventurous and courageous Native Americans had a deep respect for Mother Earth's abundantly rich natural resources. They strove to live in harmony with Her . . . never seeking or taking more than they needed to survive. This character trait would sustain their way of life for thousands of years and leave a legacy for future mankind to aspire.

SARTAYA

CHAPTER 1

One early morning on a late spring day, Nonca, whose name meant Squirrel Chaser because of her habit of wandering away from camp to pursue squirrels and other small animals, had once again strayed away from the adults of the Natayeh—*people of the Gray Wolf tribe*.

"Where have you run off to this time? Don't wander too far!" an older woman called out.

Nonca heard the calls of the old woman but chose to ignore them. She had heard the muffled cry of some creature she didn't recognize and wanted to investigate it while the adults were busy gathering edible plants. She couldn't quite make out from what direction the sound was coming. Only eight summers old, Nonca didn't know how to track animals yet. But, through trial and error, she eventually stumbled onto the source of the strange sound.

A small, male wolf-pup curled against his mother for protection, trying to hide in her fur. Trembling with fear, he couldn't understand why his mother had not attacked this strange-looking intruder. He nudged against her, again and again, crying silently for his mother to save him. But she didn't respond.

Several days before, while chasing a plump rabbit, she fell down a steep embankment onto the rocks below. She had followed the rabbit as it made a deadly error in judgment and leapt to its death down the same embankment. The mother wolf had many bruises, but it was a punctured lung from a broken rib that would eventually end her life. She had just enough strength to return to where she had hidden her small pup. That night, by the time she returned, her life force was all but drained from her mortally injured body.

She was at death's doorstep when Nonca reached down to touch what appeared to be her lifeless body. The young girl sensed that the mother wolf was very close to joining her ancestors. Loneliness for the wolf pup filled her heart as she bent over to pick it up. She cradled it in her arms against her warm chest. Suddenly, the mother wolf turned her head and bit deeply into the flesh of the girl's left forearm. Surprised by the wolf mother's attack, Nonca couldn't draw breath to scream. The wolf mother looked directly into her eyes with a sense of desperation and, then just as suddenly, released Nonca's arm. Her head fell onto Mother Earth while her life force quietly slipped away.

Nonca's arm bled from the deep puncture wounds caused by the wolf mother's unexpected bite. But she sensed the wolf pup's mother had taken her last breath.

The wolf pup whined in her arms.

"There now," Nonca whispered. "You'll be safe with me. I won't let anything hurt you." The pup sensed a mixture of fear and love from this strange being. The warmness of the stranger's body and the feel of a heartbeat as Nonca held it closer soon eased the pup's fear. It was almost the same feeling the pup had whenever it had snuggled close to its mother's belly.

While the Natayeh were used to Nonca disappearing at a moment's glance, she had now been gone for some time.

"Nonca hasn't answered me. Have any of you seen her?" the older woman asked the others. They paused in their search for food and started looking for any sign of the young girl. *It has only been a short while since we've last seen her, or has it been longer?* Just as they put their baskets of edible plants and mushrooms on the ground to begin searching for her, she strutted into view with her prized find.

"Come closer and show us what you found this time," one of the curious women playfully asked.

Nonca smiled broadly and held up the young wolf pup for all to see. Their smiles immediately turned to frowns. Then the women gasped as they realized the seriousness of the situation.

"A wolf pup!" exclaimed one woman. "The mother and father wolf will certainly not be too far behind."

"Oh, you're bleeding!" said another. "Quick! Put it down and run back to camp!"

Nonca's grandfather, Wakishtay—*Hunting Wolf*—raised his hand to calm them. "Wait. Don't panic. Pick up your baskets and walk back to camp. I will see to my granddaughter's safety."

While the others left as quickly as they could without running, Wakishtay smiled at his bewildered granddaughter. "Let me take a look at your arm. Did a wolf bite you?" The girl nodded. "I'll wrap the wound to stop the bleeding, but when we get back to camp make sure you show your wound to Maskanini and your Grandmother Miantra."

"Where did you find the wolf pup?" he asked. The girl, puzzled why everyone was so fearful, pointed in the direction from which she had just come.

"Alright, for now, we'll return to camp." Wakishtay walked Nonca and the wolf pup she held close to her chest back to their tribe's camp. He asked several women to look after the girl and the wolf pup until he returned. Then, he headed back to where Nonca had showed up with the wolf.

He soon retraced his granddaughter's tracks close to where the mother wolf had taken her last breath. "Ah. Just as I thought," he said. "If the wolf pup's mother had been healthy . . . ." He shuddered at the thought of what could have happened to the little girl who filled the emptiness of his heart with joy.

As he approached within a hundred paces of the mother wolf's final resting place, a cold but familiar instinctive chill stopped him in his tracks. All of his hunting experience told him to wait in the thicket of trees and bushes. For what, he didn't know. Then, after a few long moments, he saw it. Fortunately, he had positioned himself downwind of the place where the pup's mother had died.

A very large and majestic, black Great Gray Wolf approached the area where he had left his mate and their new wolf pup several days earlier. Catching the scent of humans, he paused, then bared his teeth and growled while glancing around for any signs of them. Seeing none, his head drooped and he gazed at the body of his mate. He smelled death on her. Gently, he nudged her with his nose, then placed a front paw on her body as if caressing her. He licked her thick and beautiful, light gray fur coat.

He carefully walked around her, as if looking for some clue that would help him understand what had happened. Then the wolf raised his head to the heavens and lost himself in an uncontrollable howling. The painful sounds emanating from deep within his belly pierced the air for miles. His anguished cry continued until he finally collapsed at her feet. The old hunter, watching nearby, now heard only a whimper.

The wolf stumbled to his feet and looked at the body of his mate for one last time. He circled her, marking an invisible boundary with his urine, leaving a scent other animals would respect. Then suddenly he turned and looked right at the old hunter as if he knew he was there. Wakishtay felt shivers along his spine. Then, the Great Gray Wolf left her side and disappeared from sight.

Wakishtay was deeply moved. He had always had the greatest respect for his namesake, the wolves. But after seeing what few human beings had, he felt closer to them than he ever imagined he could. He understood the sadness, and devastation that the Great Gray Wolf now felt from the loss of his mate. Tears slipped down the old hunter's weathered cheeks as he recalled the loss of his own loved ones. He couldn't remember when he had felt a deeper compassion for another kindred spirit. The old hunter waited a while longer to be sure the heartbroken wolf was not coming back. *He won't be coming back, but what was that look he made in my direction?*

Wakishtay stood over the female Great Gray Wolf and, looking toward the sky, called upon the Great Spirit to welcome her home. Then, with reverence, he removed her claws and her thick, beautiful, grayish-white hide according to tribal custom. As he turned her over, he noticed the broken rib and pierced lung which had ended her life. When he finished his task, the old hunter buried her remains, leaving them in Mother Earth's care.

CHAPTER 2

Members of the Natayeh were startled and amazed when Nonca returned to camp with a very young, Great Gray Wolf pup cradled in her arms. Some feared the wolf pup's parents would retaliate by stealing one of their own young children. Maybe the girl herself would be stolen. While most of the women feared the worst, the men were impressed that this little girl was able to get close enough to a mother Gray Wolf to steal its pup and not be torn to shreds. Although wolves didn't normally attack humans, they might if their young were threatened or they were desperately hungry. The tribe anxiously awaited Wakishtay's return so he could share the rest of the story with them.

Upon returning, Wakishtay knew the tribe was worried about having a wolf pup in camp. To ease their concerns, he promised to speak at the evening campfire. Of course, that did nothing to help calm the situation throughout the rest of the day. In the meantime, the old hunter sought out the leader of his tribe and had a long conversation with him. He asked the leader to allow Maskanini to perform a very special ceremony at that evening's tribal campfire. After listening intently, the leader, who deeply respected the old hunter, gave his permission. For the rest of the day, Wakishtay stayed with his brother, Maskanini, the tribal Medicine Man, to prepare for that evening's unusual ceremony.

In the meantime, one of the older and more respected women, known for her special abilities to hear and speak with the spirits of her tribe's ancestors, as well as the spirits of animals, birds, and snakes, motioned for Nonca to follow her. This woman, named

Miantra, was Nonca's grandmother.

Miantra and her first mate, Chikowa, had a little girl who would eventually become the mother of Nonca. But shortly after Miantra gave birth to her daughter, Chikowa was killed when he fell while climbing a steep cliff.

Three full moons after the horrible accident that took Chikowa's life, Maskanini asked Miantra to share his shelter so he could take care of her and her daughter. She accepted his kind offer. Over time, they fell in love and became mates. Between Maskanini, Miantra's mother when she was still living, and the tribe's ancient healers, Miantra was taught all the skills needed to be a medicine woman. She was also the Keeper of the Sacred Walking Stick, which she had received from her mother, who had it from her mother, and so on throughout the ages.

Nonca had lived with Maskanini and Miantra since she was born. Her father, who was the son of Wakishtay, had not returned from a hunting trip several full moons before her birth. After much searching by the tribe, he was presumed to be dead. The young mother-to-be had been devastated by the loss of her mate, but she then began looking forward to having their child. The delivery was difficult and Nonca's mother died while giving birth to her. It became natural for Nonca to refer to Maskanini as Grandfather, even though he was her step-grandfather, since she had lived her entire life under his roof and in his care.

Both Nonca and the wolf pup she held tightly to her chest disappeared into Miantra's shelter.

"Let me hold the pup," the older woman said softly. As the girl handed her grandmother the pup, Miantra noticed her wounded arm. "Wait, Nonca, your arm is bleeding. How did this happen? Did the mother wolf attack you?"

"The pup's mother grabbed my arm. She didn't mean to hurt me. She was just trying to protect her pup. She looked at me strangely, then she laid her head on the ground and died."

"We have to clean your wounds right away or you'll get very sick." If the animal was sick Nonca might get the same sickness and suffer a horrible death. "Put the pup in the basket behind you so I can wash your arm." After preparing a medicinal salve from crushed Marigold leaves, Miantra covered the girl's wounds with it, then wrapped her granddaughter's arm with a thin piece of unused animal hide to help keep the wound clean.

Miantra then picked the wolf pup up and held it in her arms. The pup, by now, was delirious with fear and his stomach ached. Miantra recognized the pup's symptoms of hunger. She didn't know how long it had been since the pup had any milk but without nourishment, he would soon perish and join his mother in the Spirit World.

"Nonca, take the wolf pup and hold it close while I find some food for it."

"Is he going to be all right?"

"He's very weak. I'll do my best to find something he can drink that might provide the nourishment he needs," her grandmother replied.

Miantra knew of several kinds of tall, tubular plants with thick fibrous roots that flourished near the edges of a watery marsh not far from their camp. In the past, she had used the milky substance from these plants to make a nourishing drink for infants. She wondered whether the wolf pup would drink it. It was the only chance the animal had left.

A short time later, Miantra returned with the harvested plants.

Curious, Nonca watched while her grandmother prepared the creamy-white liquid.

While Nonca held the weakening wolf pup in her arms, the old woman dipped her finger into the bowl's contents. She raised her finger and gently forced it between the lips of the pup's mouth. It took several more tries, but finally the pup's instinctive behavior took over, and it began to suck on the nourishing finger. The fluid didn't taste familiar, but the pup was so hungry that taste didn't matter. After it finished all the liquid in the bowl, the pup drifted into a deep, much needed sleep. For now, the crisis had subsided. Nonca and her grandmother hugged one another and wiped away a few unguarded tears.

"Nonca, I want you to lie down next to the wolf pup and take a nap. You're tired and could use some sleep. Be careful though, not to crush the pup." *Her face looks flushed. She may be coming down with a fever. I hope her arm doesn't become infected. I'd better tell Maskanini about the wolf-bite. Until then, I'll keep an eye on her wound.*

While her granddaughter napped beside the small furry stranger, Miantra set out to harvest more of the life-sustaining plants. *This new and unusual addition to the tribe will need much care if it is to survive,* she thought. *I wonder if the tribe will allow a wolf to live within our camp? There is much to consider. Even so, there must be a reason why the spirits allowed this to happen.* Now that she had gathered all the special plants she could carry, the old medicine woman returned to camp and began preparing more of the pup's life-sustaining drink.

That evening, the tribal campfire was bigger and brighter than usual. Many of the Natayeh had gathered around it early so they could sit close to where they thought their leader and Wakishtay would speak. Most were filled with great anticipation. While they didn't know just what would happen, they suspected something of significance since several ceremonial bowls were close to where the leader would be sitting.

The leader of the Natayeh was a strong and proven hunter. His tracking abilities were second to none. He had been honored with the name of KiaNeeishtay—*Tracking Wolf*—during his sixteenth summer of life. Several summers later, his father KiaNatay—*Gray Wolf,* who had been the tribe's leader for many summers, died unexpectedly. Even though he hadn't sought to be leader, the tribe's elders sought KiaNeeishtay out.

He was well-respected by most tribal members for his sound advice and keen insight. He was considered fair-minded and didn't form an opinion until he fully understood both sides of an argument. He had a warm, friendly smile and a generous heart. Nearly all of the tribe held him in high esteem. Several older males, who were also proven hunters, had thought that they should have been considered for tribal leader over him. Once the tribe's elders made their decision, however, it was considered final.

KiaNeeishtay, Maskanini, and Wakishtay joined the rest of the tribe at the campfire. KiaNeeishtay welcomed everyone, acknowledged the day's unusual events, and announced there was going to be a special ceremony after Wakishtay told the story about the wolf pup. With that said, the leader sat down, and Wakishtay stood up and began speaking. He told the story just as it had happened, up to and including walking his granddaughter and the wolf pup back to the main campsite. He paused before he explained what only he had witnessed after he went back to the site of the wolf pup's dead mother. He raised his arms and hands up to the heavens, as if to ask permission to continue. Just then a flash of light streaked across the evening sky and disappeared on the horizon. The old hunter, upon seeing this sign, gave thanks to the spirits for their approval, took a deep breath, and continued with the rest of his story.

Even the seasoned hunters felt an unfamiliar lump in their throats. Tears flowed freely down the sunbaked cheeks of almost all who listened. No one seemed to care what others might think of their glistening eyes and wet cheeks.

The old hunter described what he had felt when he had watched the large, majestic, Great Gray Wolf agonize over the loss of his mate. The guttural, pain-filled howling as the Great Gray Wolf raised its head to the heavens was heard by all that evening as Wakishtay raised his head to the heavens and released a wolf-like howl unlike any they had ever heard before. And then, from a distant hill, a second gut-wrenching howl, even more pain-filled than the old hunter's, was heard. Everyone felt the same chill start at the base of their spine and dart upward, raising the hair on the back of their necks. Then, a third haunting wolf-howl pierced the night air.

Spontaneously, they grabbed one another's arms for comfort. A few moments passed and only a deafening silence remained. The deep-rooted anguish felt by the Great Gray Wolf over the loss of his mate was now burned deep inside the hearts and minds of each member of the Natayeh. They would never forget this night or their deep-felt respect for this creature. Their kindred relationship with the Great Gray Wolf was reaffirmed in all of their hearts.

The campfire started to dwindle. It was time now for the ceremony their leader had mentioned earlier. The leader of the Natayeh took a deep breath, then stood and smiled at the little girl holding a wolf pup.

"Nonca, please come forward and stand by me." Nonca was unaware that this surprise ceremony was for her and the wolf pup. Miantra had suspected its purpose, but didn't speak of it to her granddaughter. She was filled with pride at the thought of her granddaughter being honored tonight.

Maskanini had risen quickly, unnoticed by others who were still reeling from the experience of just a few moments ago. He positioned himself next to the ceremonial bowls and the leader of the tribe. Nonca continued to stand facing the Natayeh leader. He smiled affectionately at her and placed his hands on her small shoulders to reassure her that everything was alright, and that she was safe. She looked into his eyes and smiled back at him. He then gently turned her around to face the campfire.

Looking over her head, he addressed the members of his tribe. "Never before in our memory has a Great Gray Wolf been allowed to reside in our camp or even near our camp. Yet, our tribe is named Natayeh, in honor of the Great Gray Wolf. How can this be? I believe the spirits that protect us, the spirits that we pray to before we begin our hunts, and the same spirits that we ask to fill our shelters with warmth and food are giving us this Great Gray Wolf pup to reaffirm our tribes name and our destiny. We will raise this wolf pup as one of our own. This night we will honor our newest addition with a proper tribal name." The tribal leader then nodded to Maskanini.

Maskanini bent over and dipped a finger into the blue-colored paste in one of the ceremonial bowls, then another finger into the red-colored paste in another bowl. He then walked over to the young girl holding the wolf pup and gently drew one multi-colored circle upon the pup's forehead. With the proper motions and deep-voiced incantations, he called upon the ancient spirits to accept the tribal name he had selected. Maskanini then turned to the other members of the tribe and announced the pup's chosen name, "Nakia—*Wolf Brother*." The tribal members thought it appropriate and cheered.

The ceremony wasn't over quite yet. The tribal leader once again motioned to Maskanini who again dipped his fingers into the two ceremonial bowls, then stood facing Nonca. The girl was confused and looked back over her shoulder into the eyes of KiaNeeishtay searching for some explanation of what was going to happen next. He smiled at her, then looked over her head and addressed the assembly.

"This girl who stands before me, known as Nonca, was chosen by the spirits to honor our tribe with a very special gift. She has brought us much luck in the form of a Great Gray Wolf pup, which we have now named Nakia and welcomed into our tribal family. This girl will no longer be known as Nonca."

Maskanini then gently drew one multi-colored circle, using both of his fingers, upon the young girl's forehead. This circle, of the two colors blue and red, meant that she and the wolf pup were related in spirit. Again, he called upon the ancient spirits to accept the young girl's new name he had selected for her. Maskanini then turned to the other members of the tribe and announced the girl's chosen name, "Sartaya—*Wolf Sister.*"

Never before had the members of this tribe, nor any other tribe, ever been witness to a ceremony that physically bonded a member of a tribe to a live wolf. *Sartaya.* The wolf pup, named Nakia, would be raised with the girl. They both would be cared for by the girl's Grandmother, Miantra, and her mate, Maskanini. All who were assembled cheered loudly and with great enthusiasm at this unique union between a wolf and a tribal member.

When the cheering died down, KiaNeeishtay raised his hands to the evening sky. "We ask the wolf mother's spirit to watch over our tribe just as she is now watching over Nakia and Sartaya." KiaNeeishtay then picked up the young girl and hugged her. "Sartaya, I am very proud of you. You may join your grandparents now."

CHAPTER 3

The young girl whose name was now Sartaya did not understand the full significance of the ceremony that had just taken place. It would take many summers before she understood how her destiny was tied to this wolf pup who was now her brother.

The next morning, after the pup was fed, Miantra took the medicinal wrap off Sartaya's arm. The wound had become crimson red but was not festering; a good sign that it might not be seriously infected. Her granddaughter's body was putting up a good fight. However, the girl's head was much warmer than normal. Sartaya's eyes were glossy and her skin seemed clammy. *She has a fever. I'm going to get Maskanini to look at her.* She found him by the stream rinsing out some of his medicine bowls.

"Let me help you with these bowls," she offered. "Then would you take a look at Sartaya? I think she has a fever from the wolf-bite."

"I'll look at her as soon as we get back. There, the bowls are rinsed now. Let's walk back together." When they arrived back at their shelter, they saw Sartaya had lain down with the pup in her arms and was almost asleep.

"Sartaya, it is the middle of the morning. Come here and let me see your wound," Maskanini said. But she barely stirred. Her grandfather went to her side and tried to sit her up. "Miantra, help me to hold her up while I check her wound."

He felt her head first and it was much hotter than when Miantra had felt her head. Her skin was damp all over her body. He uncovered her bandaged arm and saw the crimson red wound. The two puncture holes caused by the mother wolf's canine teeth were a bright red, while the rest of the wound was dark red. *Something is coursing through her body and making her body hot, too hot. I don't want her to lose consciousness.*

"Miantra, prepare a bowl of medicinal broth using the boiled leaves of the marigold to help reduce her fever. I'm going to take her down to the creek and submerge her in the water to help cool her body. I'll be back shortly with her."

After submerging most of her body in the creek for a short time, he carried her back to his shelter where Miantra anxiously waited.

"I have prepared the broth. Hold her in your lap while I try to feed her," she said. "Sartaya, wake up! You need to drink this broth. It'll make you feel better." The girl was barely conscious but with Miantra's help she managed to sip a little of the broth and swallow it. They repeated this effort several times until Sartaya slipped into unconsciousness. Miantra slipped off her granddaughter's wet garment, then asked Maskanini to lay her on the animal hide Sartaya used for sleeping. He gently wrapped the hide around her body and let her sleep.

"Submerging her cooled her down for now, but we'll have to watch her closely in case her body heats up again. If it does, I'll take her back down to the stream. And we must try to get her to drink more of the fever broth. In the meantime, I'll prepare a stronger medicine from Horsetail leaves and Ivy plants for the wound on her arm, where the fever started. If I can get the red color to go away, then most of the infection will be gone," he said matter-of-factly. "The wolf-mother's bite went deep. Sartaya will have those marks on her arm for the rest of her life."

"Do you think that the mother wolf was sick?" Miantra asked.

"I don't know. I don't want to think so. If she was, then our granddaughter will suffer greatly and we will lose her. I want to think her condition is temporary, and that our medicine will help her to get better."

Even though Sartaya was unconscious, her grandparents were able to get her to swallow more of the medicinal broth in between trips to the stream to keep her body cool. While she lay unconscious, Sartaya kept having a strange dream. She felt as if she were running with many dark animals that looked like wolves. Her dream always took place at nighttime because the sky was dark, and the moon was a pale white.

After three days, her body temperature normalized. She was still unconscious though. Finally, early on the fourth morning, she woke up from her deep sleep. Miantra and Maskanini heard her yawn, then talking quietly to her wolf brother. The girl's grandparents gazed into each other's eyes and smiled knowingly. The fever had passed.

While Miantra prepared their morning meal, Maskanini checked her wound. "Sartaya, come here so I can check your arm," he said, then smiled at her." She smiled back.

"When can I put my clothes back on?" she asked innocently.

"Wait until I check you from head to toe." He felt her forehead for any sign of a fever, but there was none. He checked her skin for dampness, but there was none. When he uncovered the medicinal wrap that covered her wound he gasped. "Miantra, come here and see her arm."

They couldn't believe what they saw. Her wound was completely healed. Even the two deep puncture holes were barely noticeable. "Those two spots where the mother wolf bit her will probably not be visible after a few more days," Maskanini said with astonishment.

"How is this possible?" asked Miantra. "I didn't expect the redness to just disappear like that. I thought she would carry the scars for the rest of her life."

"I have never seen a wound like this heal so quickly. I'm not sure what it means, but we'll check her arm each day for awhile. Sartaya, you can put your clothes on now. Let's eat."

Each day, Sartaya was reminded of the great love the wolf pup's mother had for him as she held Nakia in her arms. She soon forgot the dreams she had while she was unconscious.

Miantra began to include her granddaughter on her foraging trips for the nourishing stalks and roots for the wolf pup. In the meantime, after a few accidents and several gentle acts of discipline, Nakia quickly learned where to relieve himself outside in their shelter. Sartaya accompanied him during his frequent trips. She was to make sure he visited the designated areas when he needed it. In many cases, she used this time for herself as well.

Everyone in the tribe enjoyed holding and playing with the wolf pup. Some even got sprayed when he got overly excited and had one of his accidents. Sartaya delighted in showing off her brother to all the adults and other children. But many children harbored secret feelings of jealousy. They, too, would have loved to have such a playmate, but tribal custom had forbidden the capturing and keeping of any animals—until now. Sartaya sensed their feelings and understood how fortunate she was that the tribe had made an exception for Nakia. So, she made an extra effort to share her wolf pup with all of the tribe's children. This act of kindness did not go unnoticed by the elders. It encouraged all the children of the tribe to share their treasures with one another.

One evening, about a full moon after the ceremony took place, Wakishtay visited Maskanini's shelter to see Sartaya. The old hunter enjoyed seeing Sartaya playing with her wolf pup. This night he had a surprise for her. He handed her a very soft and pliable hide she could use to keep her and Nakia warm at night. He had worked on this hide for many days to get the pliability and sheen just right. The thick, grayish-white fur was softer than any he had ever felt before. She shrieked with happiness, startling the pup, as she jumped into the arms of the old hunter. He was satisfied that his gift was appreciated. When she placed the hide around her, she immediately sensed it was from Nakia's mother. It meant even more to her now. She couldn't wait to wrap herself and Nakia into it that night. Wakishtay bent down so she could give him one last hug and kiss before he left.

"Thank you so very much, Grandfather," she whispered. He treasured her affection and left with his reward.

CHAPTER 4

Sartaya couldn't wait until she and Nakia fell asleep that night wrapped up in the beautiful, grayish-white fur Wakishtay had given her. *That was so thoughtful of him.* She delighted in showing it off to her grandmother and Maskanini.

The older couple marveled at the fur's exquisite beauty. "You know that was a labor of love for him," Miantra said softly to her mate. His eyes glowed as he nodded. The wolf pup noticed something pleasantly familiar as soon as Sartaya placed him on the fur. Was it his keen sense of smell or the color and depth of the fur that made him remember his mother? Whatever it was, it made him yearn for her and he cried softly; his tears falling into the warmth of her fur.

Neither Sartaya nor her wolf pup had any trouble drifting off into a deep sleep. Curled up in the comfort of his mother's fur hide, Nakia enjoyed a newfound warmth and sense of security.

But just after they'd drifted off, their Dream Spirits awakened. Someone or something was calling to them. At first, it was a strange and distant sound, but then it began to sound closer. The spirit of the wolf pup recognized it first. It took the young girl's spirit a little longer, but then, it too recognized the source of the sound. "There she is. There's my mother!" exclaimed the pup's spirit. The girl's spirit saw her too.

"What a magnificent animal," her spirit gasped. All three spirits joined with one another; separate, yet together as one. A loving light, unseen by others, completely surrounded them. Their spirits filled with a sense of peace and of love and the knowledge of what had happened to the wolf pup's mother. They also understood that if they ever needed her, she would always be there for them. This strange dreamlike experience went on for quite some time. Then, the spirit of the Great Gray Wolf mother separated from their spirits and drifted away. Only the mother's beautiful gray head was visible, gazing at them while slowly disappearing into a brilliant white cloud filled with streaks of golden light. Then, she was gone from their dreams.

The sun's first rays penetrated her grandparent's shelter, hinting at the start of a new day. Miantra and her mate gazed into each other's eyes and smiled. They were the first to rise. They would let their granddaughter and the wolf pup sleep while they went about their morning routine. A little bit later, the sun's rays insisted that the rest of the camp, who were still asleep, wake up. The wolf pup stirred first, then the girl. Both felt there was something different about them this morning. At first, this unique feeling they had for one another was strange and peculiar. The closeness they felt could not be easily explained to others. This feeling would manifest itself in many ways throughout their lives. For today though, they both enjoyed one last stretch in their warm new sleeping-hide.

CHAPTER 5

The wolf pup was small compared with other wolf pups its age in the wild. This did not escape Miantra, nor did it go unnoticed by Wakishtay. Together, they decided to begin feeding the pup small scraps of meat from the tribe's kills. No one would mind sharing some of their meat with Nakia.

Wakishtay would also train the pup, along with Sartaya, on how to track and hunt smaller animals. The wolf would grow and mature more quickly than the girl. Nakia's natural instincts to hunt, kill, and eat his own prey would come soon enough. The old hunter's challenge going forward was to teach both of them the skills needed to hunt efficiently.

The first few days of training would have been frustrating for most adults. However, Wakishtay was wise enough to know he must first bond with the wolf and strengthen the relationship between his granddaughter and himself. He must gain their full trust, especially the wolf pup's before he could expect them to follow his instructions. Even though he was an old experienced hunter, Wakishtay enjoyed the boy in himself while playing with these two youngsters.

They played and took naps together for six days. This allowed the wolf pup to memorize the old hunter's scent as friendly. Actually, the pup instinctively thought of him as the leader of the pack, while Sartaya still thought of him as her other grandfather. Wakishtay did not discourage either association.

On the morning of the seventh day, Wakishtay began the next level of training. Much of their play routine involved hiding and seeking. Although still fun for the girl and her wolf, the wise old hunter began to teach them stealth. Two weeks later, the two students practiced how to walk in the forest without being heard and how to approach their prey downwind so their scent wouldn't give them away. The girl and the wolf were getting so good at approaching without being seen or heard that they thought they had surprised the old hunter one late afternoon by sneaking up on his blind side and jumping him. Wakishtay, however, had been waiting patiently for their attack. All three of them enjoyed that moment, laughing, while wrestling on the ground amid excited barks and shrieks.

By now, the three of them had formed a close bond. The wolf pup trusted the old hunter completely. Something Wakishtay did not expect, but noticed with increasing frequency, was the silent communication between the pup and the girl. A slight shifting of their bodies, a barely noticed tilting of their heads, a raised eyebrow, or a certain glare of their eyes meant something to both of them. The old hunter promised himself he would learn this unspoken language. *Imagine, I'm learning from the very two I am teaching.* After a few weeks had passed, all three were communicating with one another, without one word being spoken.

These were good days for the old hunter. Although his people treated him with the greatest of respect, he still felt emptiness in his heart since he'd quit hunting big game with the younger members. His knees, hips, and hands constantly hurt, especially after long walks or short brisk runs. In his more youthful days, he was the primary hunter of the tribe. He would bring home more game meat and fur hides than any three hunters combined. He loved everything about hunting and was the best hunter in the memory of the Natayeh. Now, he had the opportunity to pass his intimate knowledge of tracking and hunting onto the young girl, whom he loved dearly, and her wolf companion. *How fitting,* he thought as his heart filled with joy once again.

During this time, he spotted many rabbits dashing around in the woods that surrounded them. It was time to teach them how to hunt real animals. Each time he spotted signs of a rabbit, he would motion for the girl and wolf to approach. He would then get down onto his knees, and while bending down would smell the droppings from the rabbit, as well as its urine. The girl and the wolf did the same. The acrid smell sometimes made Sartaya squint and hold her breath. “Ugh! This smells terrible!” she would complain. The wolf pup seemed very interested in whatever it was they were doing and committed to memory the smell associated with different animal droppings and their urine.

On this day, Wakishtay indicated with his hands that the droppings were fresh. He followed the path left by the unsuspecting rabbit. Wherever he found a sign he immediately stopped and pointed it out to his two young companions. The wolf seemed more interested in what was going on than his sister. Sartaya’s mind wandered more often as the day grew longer. Finally, to win over the girl’s attention, Wakishtay promised they would be eating delicious rabbit meat for their afternoon meal. He also promised the fur would go to the girl if she spotted the rabbit first. From that moment on, she paid attention to the old hunter’s every observation.

I’m going to spot that rabbit first. Its fur will make warm and comfortable shoes for me. Her enthusiasm grew as the old hunter indicated they were getting closer to the rabbit. He motioned for them to be very still when they approached a clearing in the underbrush. He silently asked the girl to point out their quarry as soon as she saw it. After a few moments, she thought she saw movement behind some clumps of tall grass. She motioned to Wakishtay and pointed in the direction of the movement. The old hunter, who always carried a bow and quiver of arrows, withdrew an arrow and carefully placed the cord, which was tautly tied to both ends of the bow, into the slot of the arrow. He rested the shaft of the arrow on the arched wooden bow.

In less than three blinks of an eye, he pulled the drawstring back to his cheek, paused, and then released it. The arrow struck the rabbit just as it appeared from behind the tall grass. Sartaya shrieked with excitement, “You hit it, Grandfather! You hit it!”

The animal, which was mortally wounded, writhed in pain. Suddenly, the wolf pup scampered over to the dying rabbit and lunged at its neck. Even though the pup was still too young to do any serious damage, the old hunter was pleased that its instincts were strong. The hunter took out his flint knife and quickly slit the rabbit’s throat to end its suffering. The wolf pup upon smelling the blood, once again lunged for its neck. This time he got his first taste of fresh warm blood and loved it. Both the old hunter and the young girl laughed at the wolf pup's red covered snout. "Look at you, Nakia! Look at you with your red nose and face!" she giggled.

The wolf watched with interest while the old hunter skinned and gutted the prize of the day. Wakishtay cut several small chunks of the fresh meat and gave them to the wolf. He then skewered the remaining meat on small, freshly cut tree branches and placed them over the fire he had started. Nakia had his first taste of freshly killed meat that afternoon, while Sartaya and Wakishtay enjoyed their meat cooked.

Sartaya was delighted with the whole day. Not only was she the first to spot the rabbit they had so carefully stalked, but she also was given the rabbit hide.

"Grandfather, the rabbit meat cooked over the fire was delicious, just as you promised." She couldn't wait to get back to her grandmother's shelter to tell Miantra and Maskanini about the hunt.

That night Miantra's eyes glistened with pride as her granddaughter shared her day's experiences. Even Maskanini beamed with pride at her accomplishments. The wolf pup listened contentedly to his sister's account. He, too, was excited about the day, especially when he remembered the taste of fresh warm blood and raw meat.

Meanwhile, Wakishtay was tired and his bones ached. He began to excuse himself from all the excitement when Maskanini reached out and handed him a small pouch made of beaver hide. "The medicine will help relieve your pain and help you sleep tonight," he said with a smile. The old hunter thanked him. Later in the evening, he took some of the contents from the pouch and chewed and swallowed them with the help of water. He was tired, but very content. *The day went well. There will be many more tomorrows, and I will teach Sartaya and Nakia everything I can. Oh, yes, and I will also learn much from them.* It didn't take long for the old hunter to drift off to a deep sleep and dream the dreams that great hunters dream.

The next day, after they had eaten their morning meal, the three of them left camp in pursuit of their next quarry.

"Will we be hunting rabbit again?" Sartaya asked. "I really liked the taste of cooked rabbit meat."

The old hunter smiled. "We will follow the trail the spirits leave for us. It may be rabbit or it may be something else." She and the wolf could hardly contain their excitement.

Once the three of them were a little more than six miles from camp, the tracks of many different animals were seen. The old hunter had one particular animal in mind, though. He knew from watching wolves during some of his hunts, that they sometimes hunted beaver. He led the girl and wolf toward one of the many nearby lakes in hopes of tracking and killing one or two beavers. It would be good for the wolf to become familiar with them. In addition, beaver pelts were prized by the women of the tribe.

It took nearly half the morning to finally get to the lake the Natayeh called Ebisconni—*Sparkling Water*. In the late morning, the shining surface of the lake caused by the sun's reflection almost blinded them.

Wakishtay motioned for them to stop and rest on a cliff overlooking the water's edge. He warned them to be very still so they could observe the birds and the animals that lived in this area without being seen themselves. He pointed out the many mounds of wood sticks and branches spaced throughout the streams that emptied into and out of the lake.

As their eyes adjusted to the scenery, they saw the great multitudes of wildlife that lived in and around the lake. There were thousands of shadows swimming just below the surface of the lake. Hundreds, if not thousands, of geese floated on the surface, as well as ducks of many different features and colors. Seagulls swept down from the sky at great speeds scooping up small fish near the surface in their yellow-orange beaks.

After awhile, the old hunter spotted several beavers swimming toward shore, their flattened tails propelling and steering them. He pointed toward the beavers, but the young girl and her wolf had already seen them. Cautiously, the three worked their way around to where two beavers were heading toward shore.

Suddenly, the wolf stopped. The old hunter and the girl also stopped. None of them moved a muscle while they scanned the terrain ahead of them, searching for any possible movement by the beavers. They saw nothing, but heard the beavers gnawing on several birch saplings. The small trees shuddered as they fell to the ground. Wakishtay motioned for the wolf to circle around behind the beavers in order to cut off their escape route back to the water. He motioned for Sartaya to wait for his signal and then to make much noise. He then carefully positioned himself as close as he could to where the beavers had just cut down two of the young birch trees.

Wakishtay gave Sartaya the signal to make much commotion. "Hy, yi, yi, yi, yi!" she screamed as loud as she could. The two startled beavers abruptly stopped what they were doing and headed straight back to the water on the same path they had used earlier to get to the stand of birch trees. The last thing they expected to see at the water's edge was a young, growling wolf with bared teeth. They turned around in terror, confused about which way to run. During that brief hesitation, two arrows found their mark and the beavers dropped in their tracks.

Nakia stood over them, growling, teeth still bared. The old hunter quickly drew his knife and cut their throats so the wolf pup could indulge his instincts. He motioned for the wolf to attack. It took a lot of restraint on the wolf pup's part to wait until he was given permission to attack by the old hunter, the leader of his pack. He immediately thrust himself toward the neck of a dead beaver. Once again, the whole front of his face was covered with the blood of a kill.

Wakishtay made short work of gutting and skinning the two beavers and of cutting a handful of small chunks of meat for the wolf to eat. Nakia was in his glory. Not only had he helped his pack in killing the two beavers, but he was rewarded with the first portions of meat from the joint kill. He raised his head and howled with delight. The girl and the old hunter started a fire and cooked a small portion of the beaver meat for themselves.

Wakishtay had promised Sartaya he would cure the beaver pelts and give them to her once they were finished. Beaver pelts were held in very high regard by all tribes and often sought after when trading. The pelts were used in clothing, head coverings, wraps, and leggings.

The young girl thought the meat of the rabbit tasted better than the meat from the beaver. But it was still good.

Once again, Sartaya couldn't wait to share their adventures with her grandmother and Maskanini. However, she would have to wait until early evening when the three of them arrived back at the main camp. Once there, Wakishtay cut the beaver meat into many small portions. He then instructed Sartaya to deliver them to several of the hunters and their families who had shared meat from their kills with the wolf. Afterwards, the young girl, the wolf, and the old hunter once again entertained Miantra and Maskanini with their day's adventures. After a short time, Wakishtay excused himself to go back to his own shelter. Maskanini and Miantra smiled warmly and wished him a good night.

Wakishtay returned their smile and went to his own, empty shelter. Not only did his bones and joints ache, but his heart ached, as well. His shelter was now barren and lifeless. There was a time when it was filled with the loving warmth of his mate, Waawaatesi, and many visits by his son and his new mate. Those were happy days in the old hunter's life. Then, one day, Wakishtay's beloved mate had not awoken from her sleep. He was desolate for a long time afterward. Then, his son shared with him that he and his mate were going to have a baby. This news brought joy to the old hunter. But shortly after the announcement, tragedy had struck again. His son had not returned from a hunting trip. The tribe, after thoroughly searching for him, finally concluded that he must have met a terrible fate with a large mountain lion or bear and been carried off. Then, just six full moons later, his son's mate gave birth to a beautiful baby girl. However, the loss of her mate, her pregnancy, and her difficult delivery was too much for her heart. She died shortly after giving birth to a baby girl. That baby girl, his granddaughter, was the girl now known as Sartaya. He welcomed the deep sleep that would help mask these painful memories.

Throughout the rest of the summer, the three of them tracked and killed many small animals and birds. There were more rabbits and beavers, of course. There were also squirrels and muskrats. There were even quail, geese, and ducks. They treated themselves to the eggs of these birds as well. The Gray Wolf tribe looked forward to their return each day and enjoyed the variety of meats from their successful hunts. Rarely were Wakishtay, Sartaya, and Nakia seen apart. By now almost every family had received meat, pelts, and handfuls of colorful feathers from one of this trio's many successful hunts. Sartaya saw to that. She delighted in handing out the highly prized gifts from their exclusive hunting adventures.

It did not escape anyone's attention how fast the wolf pup was growing. Nor could anyone help but notice how exceptionally close the three of them were. The wolf pup was not only well-trained, but was also very protective of the other two members of its pack. The bond between the girl and wolf was based on a deep and special love for one another; while the relationship between the old hunter and the wolf was one of mutual respect. The old hunter considered the wolf a quick learner, a good hunter, and the girl's future protector. Wakishtay was proud of his namesake.

But Miantra now began to insist that Sartaya remain with her and not hunt every other day. This wasn't received well by her granddaughter, but the old hunter appreciated the rest. It also provided him with time to cure some of the animal skins and work on his favorite project. He was secretly making Sartaya a small bow and quiver with arrows, as well as a flint-stone knife and sheath. This was going to be a surprise gift to her when the tribe celebrated her ninth summer of life. He had discussed these gifts with Miantra and Maskanini and received their permission before starting work on them.

Miantra, on the other hand, wanted to begin teaching her granddaughter how to identify, gather, and prepare other foods besides meat. She wanted her granddaughter to be well-rounded. Throughout the next several full moons, she taught Sartaya how to cook using the various roots and leafy vegetables they had gathered. She even taught her granddaughter some of the medicinal uses of the plants that were plentiful in the area. She also taught her how to cut and sew the different fur pelts and hides into clothes, shoes, and head coverings. But she made sure her granddaughter had ample time to play and bond with the other children of the tribe. After all, Sartaya was just like every other child her age, even though she happened to have a wolf for a brother and knew more about hunting than any of the children she played with.

Her granddaughter's fever and unconsciousness from the mother wolf's bite was fading from Miantra's memory. It appeared her granddaughter suffered no long-term effects from the incident. *I am so happy Sartaya is well. It could have been so much worse. Still, it seems strange there are no marks on her arm to show where those two deep punctures were.*

CHAPTER 6

The old hunter finished the bow, quiver, and arrows, as well as the flint-stone knife and its sheath several days before the tribe was to celebrate Sartaya becoming nine summers old. Although the Natayeh always looked forward to each child's Celebration of Life, Wakishtay was especially excited about his granddaughter's special day. A sense of excitement filled the air as Sartaya, along with Nakia and her grandparents, Miantra, Maskanini, and Wakishtay approached the campfire. Sartaya and her brother sat next to the tribal leader, which was always considered an honor. Her grandparents took seats reserved for them next to her and their leader.

Several of the younger hunters beat a rhythmic sound from their stretched, animal-skinned drums. Then an even more enchanting sound came from a hollowed-out bone instrument with several holes bored into it. An older woman blew air into one end of the flute while her fingers moved over the holes. Blending with the sound of the drums, the song was hauntingly beautiful. This went on for a while and then with a glance from the tribal leader, the music stopped.

KiaNeeishtay stood up and spoke to everyone gathered around the campfire. "Not too long ago, we gathered at this very campsite to honor a young girl and her wolf pup. Although her parents are no longer with the living; most certainly they are with the rest of our ancestral spirits who watch over and guide us every day. From the beginning of time, the sky above us has been home to our kindred and ancestral spirits. Their sparkling lights in the evening sky, too numerous to count, remind us they are always nearby. Tonight, they join us in celebrating this young girl's ninth summer of life. Sartaya, please stand."

He then motioned to Miantra who quickly rose, then stood in front of her granddaughter. She smiled proudly and held out an old, small leather pouch. Sartaya's eyes glistened with excitement as she reached for the weathered pouch that had recently been thoroughly rubbed with waterproofing animal fat. She untied the drawstrings and reached into the hand-seamed leather, then withdrew the contents. Sartaya shrieked with delight as she opened her hand to reveal a beautiful Necklace of Age. It consisted of nine thumbnail-sized, evenly spaced, polished turquoise stones. Each stone had a hole through which a rawhide strand was laced. Inside the pouch were more of the polished stones, each with a hole. One stone would be added to the rawhide necklace each summer until she reached her fourteenth summer. At that time, she would replace this child's Necklace of Age with a Life Necklace of her own choosing, for she would then be a young woman.

"Oh. Grandmother, it's so beautiful! I love it. Thank you so very much." Sartaya hugged her grandmother. Everyone stood and cheered. Miantra's heart filled with pride and love as she looked up longingly at the stars.

"Tonight, my daughter who has joined her mate in the spirit world above us, be proud of your little girl. I have given her your Necklace of Age which was given to me by my mother. I miss you, my daughter."

Next, the leader of the tribe motioned to Maskanini. Maskanini stood in front of his granddaughter. He reached into a pocket of his garment and pulled out a leather pouch with a rawhide drawstring. He raised the pouch to the evening sky and asked their kindred spirits to smile approvingly upon his gift. He then handed the pouch to the smiling Sartaya. Excited, she loosened the drawstrings, then reached in and clutched its contents. She pulled her fist out and opened her small hand.

On her palm, lay a three-hooped rawhide bracelet containing eighteen wolf claws. Five came from each of the front paws and four from each of the hind paws. Wakishtay had taken them from the body of Nakia's mother when he had removed her hide and given them to

Maskanini.

"I had asked the spirit of Nakia's mother for help in finding a meaningful gift for my granddaughter's Celebration of Life," Maskanini said. "One evening, while sleeping, my spirit was awakened by the spirit of Nakia's mother. She whispered to my heart that she wanted Sartaya to have her claws. She showed me a vision in which she watched over both of them throughout their life's journey. This vision showed me that whenever danger threatened either the girl or the wolf pup, she would provide them with courage. She told my spirit that the bracelet would also remind Sartaya and Nakia of her strong love for her pup, and for the girl who was now his sister."

Sartaya was overwhelmed by her grandfather's gift. Tears welled up in her eyes. "Grandfather, thank you so very much. I will always wear this bracelet."

She hugged her grandfather. All present, including the tribal leader, were happy for the girl and feeling a little choked up themselves. Then, KiaNeeishtay motioned to the old hunter, who was Sartaya's other grandfather. Wakishtay stood in front of the girl and laid an old rolled-up deerskin at her feet and motioned for her to unfold it. As she unfolded the old skin, her eyes widened and she screamed with excitement. There, lying on the skin, were the most beautiful bow and arrows with their leather quiver and knife and sheath that she had ever seen; all made to her size. She fell to her knees, placed her head in her hands, and wept openly with joy; the only thanks the old hunter needed. Then, she slowly stood and they embraced. Neither said a word. Their eyes said everything. Neither was aware of the loud cheering by the rest of the tribe.

Everyone who had gathered around the campfire that night could hardly wait to wish Sartaya well and congratulate her on being nine summers old. They also couldn't wait to get a closer look at her gifts. As the last few people left the campfire to return to their shelters, the guest of honor felt tired, too. Miantra, Maskanini, and Wakishtay helped Sartaya with her gifts as they walked back to her grandparents' shelter. Nakia, who had watched the entire celebration with great curiosity, joined them. The girl hugged each of her grandparents.

"Thank you. Thank you so very much for everything," she

whispered to each of them. She then hugged Nakia and crawled into her bedding to enjoy a welcomed night's sleep. The wolf snuggled in next to her. The adults hugged one another and said their goodnights. Wakishtay was pleased with the way the evening had turned out. Being very tired, he headed for his own shelter, content with the evening's events and looking forward to a good night's sleep.

CHAPTER 7

Not long after falling into a deep sleep, Sartaya's dream mind awakened. Vivid scenes of her and Nakia, and sometimes Wakishtay swirled through her mind. She and her wolf companion seemed to be living a lifetime of experiences. Throughout her dream adventures, one familiar face always watched over her and the young wolf, Nakia's mother. Wakishtay also played an important role in many of these episodes. This made her feel warm and secure as she ventured in and out of the many adventures that seemed so real, yet mysterious. Unaware of it while she dreamed, a deep crimson glow appeared where Nakia's mother had sunk her fangs into Sartaya's left forearm. Then, by morning, just as mysteriously, it disappeared.

The morning light and the rustling about of her grandparents, going in and out of their shelter, gently awakened both the girl and the wolf. A new dawn promised a day filled with new experiences. After their morning routine, Sartaya and Nakia welcomed the breakfast that Miantra had prepared for them. Sartaya was looking forward to learning how to use the bow and arrows that Wakishtay had given her. She smiled as she remembered all the love showered on her that evening, along with her wonderful gifts. The previous night, as she and her grandparents walked back to their shelter, the old hunter had promised her he would teach her how to use the weapons, as well as how to take care of them.

Although she and Nakia were up to the task of learning all about bows and arrows and knives early that morning, much to the girl's disappointment, the old hunter hadn't left his shelter yet. He too had slept deeply; his head filled with dreams of his granddaughter, himself, the wolf, and the wolf's mother. Now, with the first part of the morning already past, he began to wake up.

He groaned. "I'm not as young as I used to be." *Oh well, at least I slept well.* His aging bones creaked as he slowly rose to his feet. *But what were those dreams of Sartaya, Nakia and his mother all about? Perhaps I'll ask my brother and Miantra. She understands animal spirits and dreams much better than this old hunter. Maybe I should ask my granddaughter about her dreams. My stomach is growling. It must be close to lunch time.*

It was early afternoon by the time Wakishtay, his granddaughter, and Nakia strode out of camp to practice using her new bow and arrows. The tribe had a dedicated field just outside the encampment for target practice. It was used often, but not kept up very well. Many arrows were lost in the high grass and the targets were seldom repaired. Therefore, the old hunter had found an embankment not very far from camp that he had spent nearly two weeks preparing just for Sartaya's lessons. Later on, when others became aware of this practice site, he planned to encourage them to use it. He would also insist that anyone who used this site repair the targets when they were finished practicing so they were ready for others to use. There were several trees, many bushes, and a small clearing just before the embankment in this practice area. There were also several bunches of long grass tied together so they resembled various large and small animals. Upon seeing them, Nakia bounded toward one of the rabbit-sized bunches of grass. The old hunter called to the wolf just in time to stop him from tearing into the throat of the grass figure. The wolf stopped and turned around, then looked directly into the eyes of his leader. With just the slightest movement of his head, the old hunter imparted the command to stay by his side and Nakia obeyed.

Sartaya spent the rest of the afternoon learning the proper way to string and hold her bow. She also learned how to hold the arrows with her fingers and place them correctly onto the smoothed wooden bow. After practicing these basic bow and arrow procedures over and over, she was more than ready to let some arrows fly. The first several dozen arrows either fell to the ground in front of her or flew wildly into the embankment. Now she understood why her grandfather had chosen this area. Nakia helped retrieve many of the misdirected arrows. It was like a game of fetch for him. In the beginning, he used up a lot of energy chasing her arrows.

The old hunter sensed when Sartaya was tiring and he didn't want her to become discouraged, so he decided to take a break from practice. He motioned for the girl and the pup to join him as he sat down on some logs he had positioned close together. The girl welcomed the rest. "I want to tell you a story about a little boy who wanted to be the very best hunter of his tribe."

"What's the boy's name?" Sartaya immediately asked.

The old hunter smiled and said, "His name was Broken Arrow."

"How did he get a name like that?'

"You'll have to wait for me to tell you the whole story." He reached into his leather carrying bag and handed several strips of dried squirrel meat from one of their earlier hunts to her and the wolf. The delicious treats helped quell the pangs of hunger stirring in each of them. "This should hold us until the evening meal," he said to the girl and Nakia.

He began his story. "Many moons ago, there was a young boy who watched excitedly every time a hunting party returned after several days from hunting white-tailed deer, elk, moose, and black bear. Usually, when they returned, the entire tribe would greet them with triumphant cheers.

"Many tribesmen would then relieve the hunters of their burden and begin removing the hides and butchering the meat. Once properly cut, the meat would be distributed in equal shares to each adult or placed in a common area to be dried or smoked for future use. Very little of the dead animals was wasted and not used.

"Usually, during the evening of the hunter's return, a ceremonial campfire and feast would be held in their honor. It was during one of these feasts that the young boy knew he wanted to become one of the greatest and most respected hunters of all time. He was eight summers old when he decided to train and hone his hunting skills until he realized his vision. From that moment on, he constantly begged the experienced hunters to teach him their tracking and hunting skills. He was fortunate in that his tribe was blessed with many skilled hunters and most of them were patient with him. He was taught how to track his prey long before he had an opportunity to use a bow and arrow. Only when he had learned to get close enough to his prey to use a bow and arrow, was he taught how to use them."

That's just what Grandfather is doing with me, Sartaya thought.

"Many full moons passed before this boy demonstrated the proper tracking skills needed to become a successful hunter. One of the better hunters of his tribe had made him a fine bow for his size. Several other highly regarded hunters made him a dozen or so arrows, while the boy's mother had made him a beautiful leather quiver to hold his arrows. He trained with several different hunters on how to use his bow and arrows. He trained so hard that he broke all of his arrows. When his teachers noticed that he needed new arrows, they all pitched in to make him some more. This went on for only a short while before the teachers' patience wore thin. They decided to teach him how to make his own arrows. After many attempts, the young boy finally learned how to make them properly It was his responsibility, from that point on, to make his own arrows whenever he ran short from breaking them. It didn't take him very long, after that, to treat his arrows with greater respect and to be more careful with them.

"Soon after he started making his own arrows, his skills in target practice improved. He now made his own targets out of tall grasses, tying them like he was taught so that their shape resembled real animals. He would aim at these targets from a variety of positions until he felt comfortable shooting his bow from any one of them. He slept with his bow and carried it everywhere he went. It became an extension of his body. This did not go unnoticed by the elders, and especially not by the hunters who had spent so much time training him.

"During one of many hunting ceremonies, the young boy was called to stand before the tribal leader. His hunting teachers all gathered around him in a circle. The boy didn't know what to think. His eyes opened wide and his face reddened from embarrassment. The Maskanini at that time stood to the side of the circled group and dipped his fingers into a bowl of thick reddish paste. He looked up toward the evening sky and called upon their ancestors to look favorably upon the naming of this young boy. The circle of hunters parted wide enough to allow the Maskanini through. He stood in front of the boy and drew the symbol of a two-pieced arrow onto his forehead. He then spoke to all present. 'This boy, who will soon be nine summers old, has become skilled in tracking and using his bow and arrows. Even though he is still quite young to be a hunter and has broken many arrows, his teachers believe his determination will, someday, help him to become one of the best hunters of the Natayeh. From this night forward, this boy's name will be Broken Arrow.' Everyone around the campfire cheered as each teacher hugged and lifted the boy for all to see.

"The boy's mother and father were very proud of their son. The father, who was a well-respected craftsman of arrowheads, spear points, and knives, presented him with one of the most beautiful knives any of them had ever seen. The handle, made of deer antler, had a broken arrow symbol carved into it. The blade was made from special flint known for its hardness and durability. His mother presented him with a leather knife sheath with a broken arrow symbol burned into the hide. The boy, who was not yet close to becoming a young man, felt tears of happiness stream down his cheeks as his mother and father took turns embracing him."

Sartaya had noticed the well-worn leather knife sheath and knife that her grandfather always wore at his side. She had noticed the two-piece arrow symbol that was burned into the knife sheath long before the three of them went hunting for the first time.

She smiled and shouted, "It's you! You're telling a story about yourself. Oh, Grandfather!" The old hunter was pleased she had picked up on his story so quickly. "You are Broken Arrow and you are the greatest hunter the tribe has ever seen. Maskanini has told me that many times," she squealed with delight. She went over to Wakishtay, the greatest Natayeh tribal hunter ever, and kissed his cheek and hugged him. "Can we go back to camp now?" On the walk back to their campsite, Sartaya asked, "Grandfather, just how many arrows did you break?" They both laughed out loud and continued their walk hand-in-hand.

He chuckled. "Too many to count."

Sartaya decided she too would strive to be one of the best trackers and hunters of her tribe. She never tired of practicing with her bow and arrows. She broke many arrows, and eventually, had to learn how to make her own, just like her grandfather had when he was a young boy. She even began gathering and tying the tall grasses to resemble various animals. Wakishtay couldn't have been more proud of her.

CHAPTER 8

Both Sartaya and the wolf constantly went to the practice field. Often, the old hunter would accompany them. He wanted to make certain she learned the basics of handling a bow. Every third or fourth day that she practiced, Wakishtay would ask the girl and her wolf to find the tracks of a certain animal. Then the three of them would track it until they spotted it. Sometimes, the three of them teamed up and the old hunter would shoot the prey. Other times, he would encourage the girl to get as close as possible to the animal. Between the girl and her wolf, they sometimes got within six paces of the animal. During this time, Wakishtay also taught Sartaya how to make and set snare traps for smaller animals such as rabbits, raccoons, and woodchucks. Because of their success with these traps, the trio brought many of these smaller animals back to camp. The tribe was more than happy to share in the bounty of their work.

Four seasons passed quickly and Sartaya, having recently celebrated her tenth Summer of Life, grew impatient and eager to shoot her first animal. Wakishtay did not think she was strong enough to pull back the string of a larger bow capable of killing animals. Her body had not yet had its growing spurt which would give her more height and muscle mass. Her current bow was just strong enough for target practice; not for killing game. She didn't let this deter her from practicing at the target range whenever she had the chance. She and Nakia would also leave the encampment, sometimes without her grandfather, in order to sharpen their skills at tracking small animals. Wakishtay and Miantra usually gave her permission for this as long as she didn't stray too deep into the surrounding forest. They felt comfortable that Nakia, now fully grown, would keep her safe.

One cloudy and overcast morning, with the fresh smell of impending rain in the air, she and Nakia headed for the forest's edge. She wanted to spend the entire morning tracking the footprints and droppings of different small animals until she could actually see them up close. In the middle of the morning when the skies began to sprinkle, she became even more determined. "This rain will make it more difficult to follow an animal's trail, but if Grandfather can do it, then we can, too. After all, it's not raining very hard," she said reassuringly to Nakia.

Nakia picked up the scent of something on the ground and followed it. Sartaya couldn't see any animal footprints, but she did see an occasional moccasin print. It didn't seem out of place since they weren't too far from her tribe's encampment. As she continued to follow the trail, she occasionally saw what appeared to be drops of blood. She also noticed leaves from the forest floor had been turned over, as if something had been dragged across it. This puzzled her, but they continued to follow this unusual trail for several miles. Nakia was well ahead of his sister. He knew he was following the trail of several humans and a recently killed animal. After another half of a mile, Sartaya called out to Nakia, "Wait for me. I can't keep up with you!"

Suddenly, she heard a muffled and painful yelp coming from just ahead. Dread filled her heart as she closed the distance between herself and the last sound she had heard from her brother. She emerged in a small area surrounded by trees where someone had cleared away most of the brush, leaving only ground cover. At first she didn't see anything, then a drop of moisture fell on her forehead. When she wiped it off with her hand, she saw blood. She looked upward and saw her worst nightmare.

"Nakia! Nakia!" she screamed. Hanging from a bent over branch high above her was Nakia with a rawhide rope around his neck. Hanging next to him was a skinned and bloody woodchuck. Nakia gasped for air while his body jerked. If he didn't already have a broken neck, he would soon die from not being able to breathe. She could not climb the large trees. She couldn't reach him with a long stick.

In desperation, she called upon the spirit of Nakia's mother to help her save him from this terrible snare trap. Her arm where the wolf mother had bitten her turned crimson red and throbbed with pain. She instinctively rubbed it with her other hand. As she did, her mind became more focused on Nakia. The only possible way to save him suddenly made itself known to her.

She pulled an arrow from her quiver and carefully placed it onto her bow. She saw the spot where the rope was tied to the bent branch from which Nakia was hanging. As she pulled back on the bow string, she hoped her small bow was strong enough for her arrows to cut the rope. Her first arrow nicked the branch and fell harmlessly to the ground. Her second arrow stuck in the soft wood of the branch next to the rope.

Nakia was running out of time and would soon be with his ancestors. Tears of frustration filled her eyes, clouding her vision. "No! I can't cry! I won't cry!" she yelled. "I can do this. I can save Nakia." she said as she wiped the moisture from her eyes. She mounted another arrow onto her bow, breathed slowly, took aim, and then released it. Immediately, one strand of the rope snapped as it was sliced by her arrowhead. She grabbed an arrow from her quiver and took careful aim. This arrow had to hit its target. She released her last arrow and it sliced part of the final strand of rawhide, before it stuck in the branch. But Nakia's still body hung by a thin strand of the material used to make the rope.

A look of horror swept over Sartaya's face as she screamed in anger and frustration. She had just released her last arrow and Nakia was going to die. The pain from the reddened area where Nakia's mother had bitten her intensified. It helped to clear her mind and she remembered her first arrow had missed its target and dropped to the ground. She had followed its downward flight so she could retrieve it.

She ran to where the arrow had fallen on the forest floor. She grabbed it and darted back to where she had been standing. She mounted the arrow carefully, drew back the bow string, took aim, breathed deeply, and then released it. The final strand of the rope snapped. Nakia fell to the ground. He landed, ungracefully, with a heavy thump and whimper. Sartaya ran to him and loosened the death-grip of the rope from around his neck. He gasped for air. As he took in several gulps, he stirred in her arms. As she looked deeply into his beautiful yellow eyes, he licked her face.

The rain fell harder, but neither one of them noticed. They had each other. They were both alive. Although one of them was limping slightly, they were happy. The skies darkened and took on an ominous look, as the clouds seemed to crouch over the forest treetops. But it didn't seem to take them very long to get back to their camp. Since everyone had already taken refuge in their shelters, no one saw the girl and Nakia as they entered the warmth of their own shelter and campfire.

Once inside, they were met with serious looks of concern by the three people that mattered the most to her. Earlier in the evening, Miantra had expressed her concern for Sartaya and Nakia to both Maskanini and his brother. The two men were putting together a search party when the skies opened up and rain fell in huge, gray, fog-like swaths that made it nearly impossible to see the shelters that were only thirty paces away from them. The two men concluded Sartaya would have sought shelter until the storm had passed. And the torrential rain would destroy any and all signs of her presence. Miantra, however, was beside herself thinking the worst had happened to her granddaughter.

"Sartaya, where have you been?" she uttered loudly, but with a sense of relief. "Come here and take your wet clothes off." She then handed her granddaughter an extra deerskin hide to warm her. "Come sit by the fire, next to me." Sartaya motioned for Nakia to join her as she wrapped the hide around both of them. The three adults noticed the wolf's limp.

"Is Nakia hurt?" Miantra asked. Sartaya began to sob uncontrollably as she wrapped her arms around her brother and nodded. Puzzled, the three adults looked at one another. They let their granddaughter's anguish run its course.

As her sobs diminished and her tears ebbed, Maskanini told her how much the three of them loved her and how concerned they were for her safety and well-being. "Tell us what happened to you and Nakia."

Sartaya slowly smiled, which pushed the remaining tears downward over her moist cheeks toward her mouth. "Nakia and I were following the trail of an animal that was bleeding. I couldn't find its footprints, only an occasional moccasin footprint. We followed the trail for a long ways. Nakia was way ahead of me.

"Then, suddenly I heard him yelp. It was a terrible sound. I ran even faster to where I thought the sound came from, but I couldn't see him. Then a drop of blood fell on my face and I looked up. Nakia was hanging by his neck from a rope that was tied around a bent branch. A dead woodchuck, skinned, was also hanging from a rope on another branch. Nakia's body was jerking around and he was gasping for air. The trees were too large for me to climb. Nakia was dying and I couldn't reach him. I remember asking his mother's spirit to help me. That's when I decided to try to cut the rope with my arrows. When I shot my last arrow, the rope broke and he fell to the ground. Why would someone do this and put such a large snare trap there? I could have been the one snared and hanging so high in the tree. Anybody, even one of you could have been caught."

"Sartaya, your arm is red where the mother wolf bit you. We thought the wound had disappeared. Does it hurt?" Miantra asked.

"Not anymore. But it really hurt just after I asked Nakia's wolf mother to help me. The pain cleared my mind, and I realized I had to cut the rope with my arrows if Nakia was going to have any chance at all." The three adults looked at each other with a knowing smile.

"Sartaya, why didn't you seek shelter when the rain began to fall more heavily?" Wakishtay asked.

"Once Nakia fell to the ground and began breathing, I was so relieved and so happy I didn't notice it was raining. I just wanted to get him home as soon as possible so you could check his neck and ribs." She looked directly at Maskanini.

Maskanini felt the wolf's neck and rib cage. Nakia winced several times as the Maskanini pressed firmly on his ribs. "His neck and two ribs are bruised badly. I have some medicine that will help lessen his pain, but his ribs will be sore for many days.

"I will make some hot broth for all of us. It will help warm us up and help us relax. Wakishtay can sleep with us tonight so he won't have to go out in this weather," Miantra suggested. The brother of her mate smiled in appreciation. "I'm sure the two of you will be discussing this day's events late into the evening," she said as she glanced knowingly at the two men. They nodded and fixed their eyes on one another as their minds went over what their granddaughter had told them.

Anger filled their hearts as they thought how something much worse could have happened this day. They both remembered how, many generations ago, their ancestors had banned this kind of large snare trap because they weren't checked very often and the animals who were caught in them usually suffered for long periods of time before they died. Occasionally, an unsuspecting tribal member or a member from another tribe would become a victim of these lethal traps. The punishment for setting and using such a snare trap was usually very severe. It was for these reasons that no one from the Natayeh had used such a trap for generations. Now someone had violated that ban, but who would have done such a thing and why? They both wondered, as if reading one another's minds.

Wakishtay spoke first. "This is serious. We must learn who did such a thing and why. Maskanini, you and I must speak with KiaNeeishtay this evening. After we tell him what's happened, we'll ask him what he thinks we should do next. Sartaya, do you think you can lead some of us back to the area where the snare trap is?"

"Yes, Grandfather, I'll never forget it. Nakia can also help, if he's up to it. Will we be going first thing tomorrow morning?"

"I hope that KiaNeeishtay will want several of his most trusted men to go with us as early as possible; maybe even before the sun is awake. It will be difficult for you to show us where Nakia was almost killed, but I know you can do it."

The two men grabbed the hides they had wrapped around themselves and placed them over their heads as they left their shelter for KiaNeeishtay's. The rain poured down as they announced themselves at the entrance to the shelter of the Natayeh leader.

"You may enter, Maskanini and Wakishtay." The two visitors

secured the deerskin flap behind them to keep the weather out of the shelter. "Join us at our fire and warm those old bones," KiaNeeishtay said with a smile. "Miikwasi will warm us with some hot broth." After noticing the serious looks on his visitors' faces, he added, "I suspect we will be here for quite awhile." His mate, Miikwasi, nodded and began to prepare the broth.

"What brings you to my shelter on such a miserable night?"

Maskanini spoke first and told the story just as Sartaya had told him, Wakishtay, and Miantra. "Is Sartaya or Nakia hurt?" KiaNeeishtay asked.

"Nakia has bruised ribs from the fall and cuts on his neck from the rope. It is painful for him to lie down and it's difficult for him to swallow. Sartaya is still reeling from almost losing her brother," Maskanini replied. The others nodded.

"Can your granddaughter lead us to the area where the snare trap is located?" their leader asked.

"Yes. She suggested Nakia come with us as well." Maskanini answered.

"Wakishtay, what are your thoughts about what happened and what we should do about it?" KiaNeeishtay asked the old and respected hunter.

"With your approval, I think we should take you and one of your most trusted men with us just before daylight tomorrow morning, depending on whether the rain stops. We should be careful not to alert anyone who may have had any part in this snare trap. Whoever is involved may want to check on their trap after their morning meal, so we should be careful and hide ourselves around the area before then."

"That is a good plan. I will speak to Lakato about going with us. It will be you, Wakishtay, Lakato, me, Sartaya, and Nakia who will go. Maskanini, I want you and Miantra to stay here and spread the word that Sartaya is missing and how concerned you both are that your granddaughter and Nakia did not come back to your shelter last night. Maybe that will cause the guilty one to check on the snare trap. Many others will want to help you in searching for Sartaya and Nakia. You must stall them by telling them you will wait until the afternoon to begin looking for her." Maskanini nodded.

The rain stopped sometime during the night. Early the next morning, before most of the Natayeh began to stir from their warm sleeping hides to rekindle their fires, KiaNeeishtay and the others were already well on their way. At first light, Maskanini and Miantra made their rounds from fire pit to fire pit lamenting their concerns over their granddaughter being missing. The couple kept their eyes opened for anything unusual. Everyone seemed to be sympathetic and offered their help to search for Sartaya, except for two families on the far side of the encampment. The families, and especially two older boys, seemed to be less interested in their story then most everyone else in the tribe. Once the couple had left these two families to go on to the next shelter, both Maskanini and Miantra noticed the two older boys hurriedly left the encampment.

Miantra and Maskanini knew very little about these two families. They did know, however, that they were not permanent residents of the Natayeh. Miantra and Maskanini decided to gather more information about them. What they learned was troubling.

These two families were distant relatives of one of the Natayeh families. They had arrived unannounced the previous summer after traveling more than two full moons from their own tribal grounds southwest of the Natayeh camp. Their initial plan was to stay for the summer and then return to their own tribe in the fall. Instead, they stayed through the winter and spring with no signs that they were eager to return back to their own tribe.

They had gladly accepted the graciousness of their distant relatives and of their hosting tribe. Early on when they first arrived, tribal members helped them to build two shelters and provided them with meat from tribal hunts. The visitors, on the other hand were lazy gatherers and incompetent hunters who offered nothing in return to the Natayeh or to their distant relatives. They rarely attended tribal campfires or tribal hunts. Their two boys never mingled with other boys their own age. Eventually, the burden of feeding these two families fell upon their distant relatives, as others stopped their donations of food. Some had begun to wonder whether these two families really had a tribe to go back to, or whether they were outcasts.

As Miantra and Maskanini probed deeper into these guests who had overstayed their welcome, they became very disturbed by what they heard. Several families whose shelters were fairly close to the unwanted guests' shelters had often overheard them complaining about the attention given to the orphan girl and her wolf. These two families considered an orphan the lowest of the low. They also thought Miantra and Maskanini were living in filth by having a wolf and the orphan girl with them in their shelter. They were also heard complaining about older people and how the tribe would be better off without them. During many of these outbursts, they mentioned the names of many respected elders including Wakishtay, Maskanini and Miantra and suggested they be taken into the wilderness and left to die so the tribe would not be burdened with feeding and caring for them.

Miantra and Maskanini finally looked at each other and nodded. Their search was over. They had found what they were looking for. Now, they needed to get back to their shelter and wait until the others returned from their trap.

Sartaya and Nakia led the special group close to the snare trap. They remained outside of the immediate area so as not to alert whoever might have set the trap if they happened to come around during the morning to check on it. The three men immediately noticed the four arrows embedded into the high, bent-over branch and nodded to one another in amazement at the girl's accuracy. They also saw the skinned woodchuck tied to another high branch. The animal's skinned carcass had been dragged along the ground to lure the wolf to this spot. The three had agreed only sign language was to be used in case someone else was close by. KiaNeeishtay motioned to each of them where they were to position themselves. Each man found plenty of cover to hide from view. Wakishtay would approach whoever might show up.

They only had to wait a short while before they heard the noisy approach of two boys. The boys appeared to be about fourteen to sixteen summers old and were carrying spears, bows, and quivers full of arrows. They entered directly underneath the sprung trap and looked up.

"Where is she?" one of the boys yelled.

"Where is the wolf?" the other boy shouted. "Look at the arrows stuck in the branch. The trap must have caught the wolf and she cut the rope with her arrows. But where is she? She never went back to her shelter. Where could she have gone?"

"She couldn't have shot those arrows with her small bow!" the first boy yelled back. "Someone else must have shot them and now has her. Maybe strangers took her captive and are eating the wolf as we speak. I hope that's what happened, so she gets exactly what she deserves. You know what would happen to that orphan girl if she was taken captive, don't you?"

The other boy nodded. "We've missed our chance to get rid of her and her filthy animal. She shouldn't have been part of this tribe, anyway. She's just an orphan. Anyway, who keeps an animal in their shelter, let alone a wolf? Our fathers are going to be very disappointed. The trap they helped us build didn't catch either the girl or the wolf."

Just then, they heard a rustling noise and Wakishtay appeared as if out of nowhere. "Who are you boys and what are you doing here?" he asked quietly, never taking his eyes off of them. The old hunter appeared defenseless, except for his sheathed knife. So the two startled boys thought they had the advantage over this old man standing alone in front of them.

The taller of the two boys, Fenwati, known as Catcher of Turtles because of his long, narrow neck and his penchant for catching turtles to be used in soups, snickered. "Old man, you are the grandfather of the ugly orphan girl. You never should have come here. We thought we snared her in our trap, or at least her filthy wolf. We think her wolf was caught and is probably dead; maybe even eaten by whoever found him. That is a good thing. Maybe the lowly orphan girl was taken as well. That would be even better. If not, we'll take care of her just as we did the wolf. But first, old man, we must kill you so that no one will ever be the wiser. You are worthless to the Natayeh, anyway. Your life is over and you have become a burden to all of us."

Fenwati, lifted his spear. The shorter boy, Dyoshat, whose given name was Chaser of Fire Flies because when he was younger he was always chasing and catching fire flies when in season, also wanted a part of the old man. He raised his spear and pointed it at Wakishtay.

In a flash, Nakia darted from his sister's side. He didn't realize the other men present would never allow anything to happen to Wakishtay. The taller boy never heard or saw the wolf lunge, knocking him onto his back. Pain-filled screams filled the forest as the wolf shredded his throwing arm with his powerful jaws. The boy's forearm lay open to the bone, muscles, cartilage, arteries, and nerves torn beyond repair.

The shorter boy enraged at the sight of his friend bleeding out leapt toward the wolf, ready to drive his spear deep into the animal's back, hoping to finally end its miserable, filthy life. While in midair, an arrow struck his shoulder with such force it stopped him in his tracks. He fell to the ground with a thump. He, too, screamed from the excruciating pain of the sharpened, flint arrowhead buried deep in his shoulder bone.

The arm attached to his wounded shoulder wouldn't respond as he tried to use it to stand up. As he raised himself to his knees using his other arm, he looked up and screamed when he saw the wolf in front of his face, growling and staring at him with bright yellow eyes and bared fangs stained with the blood of his friend. Sartaya and her grandfather stood on either side of the wolf. All it would have taken was a slight nod by either of them for the wolf to lunge at the boy's throat and end his life; but they didn't move a muscle. The Natayeh tribal leader and his trusted friend, Lakato, also stood on the boy's right and left side. The only sounds in the forest were the desperate moans coming from the wounded boys. Their hearts filled with dread as they began to realize what might happen to them.

Everyone's attendance was mandatory at the evening campfire. No one, except for a small group of people, knew the purpose of this specially called meeting. As the fire glowed brighter in the early evening skies, KiaNeeishtay stood and raised his hand to signal silence. His face was solemn as an ominous hush fell over the crowded campfire.

"For many generations, further back than anyone here can remember, our ancient ancestors forbade the setting of large snare traps to catch large prey. There was good reason for this. Oftentimes, the caught animal died a slow, agonizing death while hanging in the air. Sometimes, the snare trap was so powerful that it ripped the animal apart. Mother Earth was unhappy that we would treat the animals she sent to feed us with such disrespect. Her wishes were ignored for a long time. Then, some people were killed by snare traps. These accidents continued until our ancestors finally realized how very dangerous these traps were. Since that time, most tribes forbid their use.

"Yesterday, one of our own walked into one of these traps and was left hanging by his neck to die a most horrific death." Everyone gathered around the campfire gasped in horror. "Nakia's sister couldn't reach the rope to free him as it was tied on a bending branch very high in the trees. The wolf's own weight made him choke as the snare closed tighter around his neck. In desperation, Sartaya shot arrows at the branch where the rope was tied. Fortunately, her arrows flew straight and true. The rope broke and Nakia fell to the ground. Look around this campfire. See your mates, your children, and your friends. This could have happened to any one of them, or even to you. This time, it happened to Nakia and it was Sartaya who saved her brother from a most painful death."

KiaNeeishtay allowed time for his people to digest what he had just said. There was much loud talking and shouting as the full meaning of what he had just shared with them began to sink in. "We have caught those responsible for setting the snare trap. The two boys did so to catch either Sartaya or Nakia, or both of them at the same time. And, sadly, they were encouraged and helped by their parents.

"These people were welcomed by our tribe as our guests last summer when they first arrived unexpectedly to visit with their distant relatives. They claimed they had come from a tribe several full moons travel to the southwest. I'm not sure they belonged to any tribe. Our people treated them with respect and helped them in many ways. They returned our generosity by breaking our laws and trying to kill two of us."

Again, the Natayeh leader paused. Again, there was an outburst of anger by his tribe. KiaNeeishtay had to raise his hand demanding silence. He motioned for Wakishtay, Maskanini, and Lakato to position themselves evenly around the campfire to maintain order and help calm everyone.

"Their fate has already been decided by myself and the elders. At first, we thought they should be taken into the forest and hung by their necks just as they had plotted to kill Sartaya and Nakia. Then, we decided to ask Maskanini and Miantra what they thought would be a just response to those responsible for planning such an evil act against their granddaughter and Nakia. They calmly and wisely suggested that the two boys and their families be banned from our tribe and hunting grounds for all time. They will be branded with the banishment sign on their foreheads, so that all neighboring tribes will know them for who they are, and will not offer them any help. The elders and I thought this was a wise and just punishment. But, then, we also added that if they were to ever return for any reason, they would face a certain and swift death. This is what we have decided and this is what shall be done. Our decision is final."

KiaNeeishtay paused for a moment so that everyone had a chance to catch their breath. No one spoke a word. "We want every one of you to know who these people are so that you'll remember what happened here tonight and be able to alert us if you ever see any of them after this day's end. Their names will never be spoken again by any member of the Natayeh. I want you to form two lines on the far side of the fire. The two boys and their families responsible for setting the snare trap will pass through these lines as they leave us forever. They will leave with nothing but the clothes on their backs. Their shelters and their weapons will be destroyed and burned, tonight. It will be as though they never existed. The two families have agreed to this punishment, as opposed to the alternative, which was death."

The Natayeh leader then motioned to several of his tribesmen to send the two banished families into the space already formed by the two lines of people. The two families made their way through the space with their heads bowed in shame, trying to hide the freshly branded symbol of banishment from those standing in the lines. Each Natayeh tribal member took a good look at them, and then turned around with their back to them. This was a grave insult, but everyone agreed it was a well-deserved one.

The condition of the two wounded boys was dire. Without the proper treatment for their serious wounds, most concluded the boys would succumb to the harsh elements of an early winter's arrival. The majority of the tribe felt that punishment was more than justified. A few didn't think it strong enough. It boiled their blood to think that those traps could have snared and killed one of their own family members or friends.

Sometime toward the end of that winter's reign, the remains of the two boys who had set the snare were found by a neighboring tribe's hunting party. While visiting the Natayeh, the hunters shared with them that while the bodies they found had been pretty much destroyed by scavengers, the banishment scars were still noticeable on their foreheads. They also mentioned that while trading with a tribe whose hunting grounds were one full moon travel to the southwest, they had seen the other banished family members. The shamed families had been captured while foraging for food within this tribe's hunting grounds, and were now lowly slaves. The visiting hunters concluded their story by saying these families' lives would forever be sealed in misery. Gathered around the winter evening's blazing campfire and listening to the visitors, the Natayeh tribal members looked at one another and nodded approvingly.

CHAPTER 9

Another summer passed and the tribe celebrated Sartaya's eleventh Summer of Life. Her Grandfather Wakishtay gave her a stronger bow and a new quiver of longer arrows. By now, her proficiency in tracking and target shooting exceeded even his expectations. He promised her that as soon as she was able to master her new bow she would be allowed to make her first kill. The old hunter also felt more comfortable now that Nakia was fully grown and could protect her better than he could.

About a full moon after Sartaya added the eleventh polished turquoise stone to her Necklace of Age, she, Nakia, and her grandfather left the campsite early one morning to track and hunt a few game animals for dinner. *I wonder when Grandfather will allow me to kill an animal. After all, I am eleven summers old now, and he did give me a stronger bow. I know I can shoot my arrows straight. Will he give me the sign to kill the next small animal that we track,* she wondered. *Doesn't he trust me, or maybe he just doesn't think I'm ready yet? I'm more than ready. Can't he see that?*

Wakishtay was more quiet than usual on this beautiful morning. *Is she really ready to kill one of the animals we practiced tracking? Have I pushed her to this point too fast? After all, she is only into her eleventh summer of life, and she is a girl. Am I expecting too much from her because she is my granddaughter? What if she fails? She can't fail! But if she does, will she become discouraged and want to forget all about tracking and hunting? Still, she is stronger and more skilled than all the boys her age; even more than some older boys. I taught her well and she will do well. She is ready.*

The old hunter put all of these unsettling thoughts to rest and focused on what he knew best, tracking and hunting. Silently, he asked the spirit of Nakia's mother to watch over the three of them and guide them to a successful hunt. Of the three of them only he knew where the path, which looked like many they had taken in the past, would lead them.

Around mid-morning they approached a clearing on the top of a cliff overlooking a sparkling lake. They had hunted here many times before and had taken several beavers from its shores. Only this time, they were at the other end of the jeweled lake. The view was just as beautiful from the over-hanging cliff at this end of the lake as it was from the other.

Birds of all shapes and sizes flew overhead or just floated lazily on the lake's smooth, blue-green surface. Thousands of dark shadows darted in all directions below the water's surface. When some of these fish neared the surface, a giant white-headed and white-tailed bird swooped down from the cloud spattered sky, and snatched up one of the fish with its long, sharp talons. This magnificent creature then flew off to the nearest dead tree limb with its still-wriggling catch and proceeded to feast on it.

Wakishtay motioned to the others, then pointed to another movement near the shoreline below them. The girl and the wolf noticed several beavers building stick and mud mounds in one of the many water-ways leading to the lake. With just the slightest of motions from their leader, Sartaya and Nakia began moving down a narrow path that led to the bottom of the hill under the cliff where they had just been standing.

Once they arrived at the bottom, the old hunter quietly asked his granddaughter where each of them should position themselves for the best ambush of these beavers once they came ashore. Remaining silent, she pointed to Nakia and then to a spot that would block the beavers' retreat to the safety of the water. Next, she pointed to her grandfather and then to a clump of bushes where he could hide from the beavers' view. She then pointed from herself to a large tree where she could hide. At the right time, she would scream and make all the noise she possibly could to strike terror into the unsuspecting animals.

The old hunter was pleased with his granddaughter's answers. He would not have changed one instruction.

Wakishtay looked directly into Sartaya's deep brown eyes and pointed to the area where she had indicated he should be. She smiled when she understood he wanted her to wait in the bushes. Then, she looked into Nakia's bright yellow eyes and with the slightest head movement motioned for him to join her. Wakishtay quietly made his way to the large tree where Sartaya indicated she would wait.

They waited patiently for the beavers to return to their accustomed work area. The young girl, full of joy, prepared her bow and arrows for the kill, just like her grandfather had taught her. Nakia sensed this hunt was different from others. He knew this position in the bushes was for the hunter who would kill the animals they had tracked. He also sensed his sister's excitement.

Sartaya's mind flooded with thoughts and misgivings of every kind. *I can't disappoint my grandfather. If I miss the target, he might never take me hunting again. But what if I do miss,* she wondered. *What if the beavers don't hesitate before fleeing and I don't even get an arrow off? I know my arrows will find their mark if I get a chance to release them. I know I can do this. Grandfather thinks I can do this. Why else would he have told me to take his place as the hunter?* Sartaya called upon the spirit of Nakia's mother for help. *Mother of my Nakia, please help me to calm down and be the hunter my grandfather wants me to be. Make true my aim and guide my arrows to their target so that the kills are sure and swift, and the beavers do not suffer.*

After making her heartfelt request, the wound in her arm from the mother wolf's bite turned a crimson red and filled her with a sobering pain. As the pain throbbed, every muscle in her young body tightened. Her mind cleared of all thoughts, except for her surroundings and why she was there. Her sight, hearing, and smell became more acute. She sensed that the spirit of Nakia's mother now filled her and she was seeing, hearing, and smelling with the eyes, ears, and nose of the mother wolf. Her heightened awareness of everything around her increased her confidence in herself and her abilities. Nakia noticed the profound change in his human sister. He sensed her newfound confidence and the spirit of his mother inside her.

Wakishtay also noticed and smiled knowingly.

Sartaya's newly acquired keen senses alerted her to movement at the water's edge. She motioned to Nakia, who had also sensed the beavers coming ashore, to circle around the prey and cut off their retreat. In an instant, he had silently disappeared from her side. She then placed one of her arrows between her fingers and rested it silently on her wooden bow. She waited until the beavers were only nine paces from her position and then looked at her grandfather. He hollered and clapped his hands loudly. The startled beavers looked in his direction, then turned to run back the way they had come. One of the beavers took only two steps before being struck down by an arrow. The other, unaware its partner had fallen ran as fast as its small legs could take it toward the safety of the water. Just as it neared the water's edge a wolf, bared teeth and growling, appeared between it and the water. The terrified beaver paused in confusion, then swerved to evade the new threat. During that brief hesitation, however, another arrow found its mark.

Sartaya nodded to the wolf and gave him permission to lunge at the beaver's throat to ensure it was dead. This also allowed the wolf to practice its killing technique and satisfy its taste for blood. Sartaya's grandfather was very pleased with her and the maturity she had shown throughout her first kill. He was now convinced, more than ever, that his granddaughter was destined to not only be a great tracker and hunter, but also a great leader someday. She saw the pride in his face and she blushed with joy.

They both laughed at the sight of Nakia with his red stained snout. The girl took her wolf to the edge of the water and motioned for him to go for a swim. The wolf hesitated until she waded into the water first. They chased each other in the shallow water. After awhile, they returned to the sandy beach, soaking wet and a little tired.

Wakishtay searched for and found a strong dead branch, about the length of his granddaughter, lying on the ground. He took the top layer of his smoothed, animal-skin clothing off and wrapped it several times around the center of the stick for cushioning. It had been a long day and as they were quite a distance from their camp, he decided to gut the animals she had just killed. He promised her she could gut her next kill. With quick decisive strokes, he gutted the two beavers with his old but very sharp knife that had a broken arrow carved into its handle. He then tied a beaver to each end of the dead branch, lifted the piece of wood over his head, and rested it on his shoulders. These were not small beavers and they were heavy. *I'll be in need of some very strong medicine for my pain and to help me sleep tonight.* He motioned to his two companions to begin the hike back to camp. It took the three of them the rest of the afternoon and early evening to finally arrive back at their campsite. They had to stop several times for the old hunter to rest and reposition the heavy load on his shoulders.

By the time the small hunting party arrived back at their camp, most people had already settled into their own shelters for the night. Wakishtay took his granddaughter and her wolf to his brother's shelter. Miantra and Maskanini couldn't have been more proud of her feat and congratulated her. They noticed how tired the three hunters were and offered them a meal. Everyone ate heartily as the story of the hunt was told, then retold several more times. Nakia nodded off after laying his head on his sister's lap.

Wakishtay excused himself and left for his own shelter to skin the beavers. After he finished, he stored the beaver meat and skins in leather bags and hoisted them high above the ground onto a meat rack to secure them from any marauding animals. By now, the old hunter was tired and ready to collapse from the pain and fatigue of a very long day. He smiled gratefully when he saw his brother had paid a visit to his shelter, leaving him with a bag of medicine to help ease his pain and help him fall asleep.

CHAPTER 10

Sartaya's grandmother woke shortly after dawn. This particular morning she decided to let her granddaughter and Nakia sleep later into the morning. *They both need the extra rest after yesterday's long hunting trip.* As she gazed down upon her sleeping granddaughter and the wolf lying next to her, she wondered what the future held for them.

This girl of only eleven summers, and who has a wolf for a companion, is already an accomplished tracker and hunter, thanks to my mate's brother. But she must also learn how to identify and prepare other foods besides meat. I also need to keep teaching her the medicinal value of different plants and how to make clothes and shoes and head-coverings. She still has so much more to learn. But for today, I will let my granddaughter rest and enjoy the excitement from her first kill. Everyone will be asking her to tell the story over and over. With visions of many happy tomorrows spent with her granddaughter swirling around in her mind, Sartaya's grandmother slipped through their shelter's deer-hide entrance flaps.

As the rising sun became more insistent that everyone should be up and going about their morning chores, the girl and her wolf finally stirred. Their eyelids were full of sleep-dust and still heavy from many adventurous dreams. Nakia rose first, then he bent over to lick Sartaya's cheeks, encouraging her to rise also. They both poked their heads out of the shelter and were greeted by the brilliant rays of the sun. A beautiful morning promised to become a spectacular day.

After their regular morning routine, Sartaya splashed some cool water toward Nakia and onto her face from the fast running stream that raced past the outer northeast edge of the campground. From there, they made their way back to the campfire just outside their shelter. The girl's grandmother had kept breakfast warm. Several hunters had already returned from hunting smaller game that morning and had dropped off some chunks of raw meat for which Nakia was noticeably grateful.

After she had finished her breakfast and helped her grandmother with some morning chores, she asked Miantra if she could look in on Wakishtay. "I want to make sure he's feeling well, and ask him if he needs any help with anything. He was really tired last night. I felt badly for him because I knew he still had to skin the beavers before he could finally rest his eyes for the night."

"No, leave him rest for as long as he needs to. He'll be up before too long. Why don't you go play with the other children and tell them about your first kill yesterday? I'm sure they are all excited to hear how you and Nakia helped your grandfather track and kill those two large beavers."

"All right. But will you tell me when Grandfather is up? I want to ask him something very important."

She probably wants him to teach her how to gut and skin the animals she kills, Miantra surmised.

The other children gathered around Sartaya and her wolf companion as she eagerly made her way toward them. Many squeals of excitement could be heard coming from the group of wide-eyed children as she proudly shared the events of her first kill.

One boy, a few summers older than Sartaya, listened quietly, but could not bring himself to congratulate her and share in her excitement. Yukawe, filled with envy, wished Sartaya had never been born. *This should be me telling the others about one of my many kills. Why is she always the center of attention?* He left the group, unnoticed, more determined than before to come up with a spectacular kill that would get the attention of the entire tribe. He imagined himself surrounded by his proud parents, the leader of their tribe asking him to tell his story to the rest of the tribe at a special celebration campfire for him. Later in the evening, when he was having dinner with his parents, his father asked him if he had heard about Sartaya's good fortune. The boy's eyes glistened and his heart ached with shame. "Yes, Father, I heard."

Two summers ago, his father, Lakato had given him a bow and arrows to hunt small game. A strong bow, capable of felling most animals, he had presented it to his son during the celebration of his eleventh Summer of Life. Yukawe could outrun most of the other children of the tribe. Yet, now into his thirteenth summer, he still had not killed his first animal. *I'm a failure at hunting and my father is very disappointed in me.*

Lakato was famous for the spears he made. He used the hardest of woods to make the shafts, and a very hard, amber-colored flint, not commonly found near the Natayeh encampment, to craft the sharp spear point. His skill at making straight, well balanced, customized spears was well known throughout the region. Not only were they made from the finest materials, but he customized each one to the size of the individual receiving it. He carved images of animals and birds into the upper half of the wood, along with a symbol for the given name of the recipient.

Lakato never felt disappointment or shame in his son. He loved him with all his heart. He did wonder, however, if he should have waited several more summers before giving Yukawe such a strong bow.

A few days after Sartaya's first kill, Yukawe, determined to bring home a kill, took his bow and quiver of arrows to the practice site created by Wakishtay. He made sure he was alone because others now practiced at the site. Whenever he put a reasonable distance between himself and the grass-shaped targets, his arrows missed their mark. "What is wrong with me? Why can't I hit the targets?" he shouted angrily.

"Maybe your bow is too large and strong for you," another voice quietly said.

It was Sartaya and Nakia. "What are you spying on me for?" He was angry and embarrassed.

"I'm not spying on you. After all, this practice area is for everyone, I just came here to practice . . . like you did. I noticed though, how hard it is for you to hold your bow still once you've drawn the arrow back. I know I couldn't hit anything if I couldn't hold my bow steady," she continued. "May I try your bow?"

Frustrated and disgusted with himself, he threw his bow to the ground. *Now I suppose she'll tell everyone in camp what a horrible shot I am.* Sartaya picked up the bow, then holding it firmly she tried to pull it back.

She gasped. "I can't even get it half-way back to where it should be. Yet, you can pull it all the way back."

"Yes, but I can't hold it steady once I have," Yukawe replied. "I think you're right about it being too strong for me. But I don't want to disappoint my father. He made this beautiful bow for my eleventh Summer-of-Life celebration."

"Yes, I remember how many compliments you received about your bow." She held hers out to him. "Try mine. It might be too easy for you, but give it a try." Yukawe reluctantly took her bow. He placed an arrow on the bow and pulled it back easily. Without any effort at all, he held it there, took a deep breath, and released it. The arrow found its mark with ease. Yukawe, surprised by his own accuracy, couldn't have been happier.

"It wasn't me. It was the bow, all this time. How will I ever tell my father without him feeling I don't appreciate his gift?"

"Tell him the truth. He'll understand. Maybe, he'll even make you another bow, but one more for your size. Tell him you look forward to the day when you can use this stronger bow." She smiled. "Nakia and I are going hunting tomorrow. Would you like to go with us? You can use my bow and arrows for the kill."

Yukawe swallowed hard.

"You know, I was really jealous when you came back to camp with your first kill. Terrible thoughts went through my mind. I was just thinking of myself. I'm sorry. Can we be friends? And yes, I would really like to hunt with you and Nakia. Thank you so much for asking me." Smiling, Sartaya nodded. The next day, after breakfast, the three of them met at the edge of their tribe's encampment to begin their hunting adventure.

Nakia was not used to strangers joining him and Sartaya when they went hunting. He planned to stay closer to his sister than he usually did, in case she needed his protection. Half way through the morning, they approached a field of tall grasses. Nakia signaled Sartaya there was game in the field. Sartaya told Yukawe, with a hand signal, to stop. When he started to speak she put her fingers to her lips. She gave Yukawe her bow and arrows, then motioned for him not to move. Then, she signaled Nakia to position himself behind whatever it was that he had sensed, so he could flush it towards them. The boy and girl crouched down so as not to be seen by the prey until it was too late.

Nakia growled and leapt toward a cluster of high grasses. The startled bird, a large male turkey, ran right toward the hunters. Yukawe quickly pulled the arrow back to its proper position on the borrowed bow, took a quick deep breath, and then released the arrow. The turkey, fatally struck, took several steps sideways, stumbled, then fell. It never saw the weapon or the hunter that ended its life. It was a quick, clean kill with the arrow piercing its heart. Nakia immediately made his way beside the large bird. He waited for his sister's signal to ensure the bird's death by gripping its neck and ripping its throat. She obliged him. Yukawe witnessed the ritual and understood its meaning. He was so elated to finally have his first kill. He couldn't wait to show his father and mother. After finding two long sticks, he secured the turkey between them, and resting the ends of the sticks on his shoulders, dragged his prize behind him.

Lakato and Bosaata couldn't have been prouder than when their son strode into camp, with his first kill. All the children rushed toward Yukawe who had reached his family's shelter. Dozens of questions pummeled the young hunter. He graciously answered each and every one of them. He had never before felt more proud of himself than he did at this moment. Later that evening, he told his father the entire story. Lakato promised his son he would make him a new bow; one that would let him hunt successfully. Before Yukawe slept that night, he remembered how Sartaya had made it possible. He vowed to repay her good deed and as he drifted into a well-earned slumber, he suddenly knew how he would repay her kindness.

After checking with Sartaya's grandparents for their approval, it took Lakato a handful of sunrises to oblige his son's request to make Sartaya a spear. He customized it to her size and carved the image of a wolf's head on the upper half of the wooden shaft. He made the spearhead out of the finest blue-and-gray flint of the region. Its edges were razor sharp. When he finished Sartaya's spear, he made another one for his son, but did not tell him. He was proud of Yukawe for not thinking of himself when he had asked his father to make a spear for her to show his gratitude for her gracious help. Lakato wanted to reward his son for his unselfish request.

Yukawe didn't understand why it was taking his father so long to make the spear. Seven days later, when his father presented her finished spear to him, he understood. It was the most beautiful spear his father had ever made. The walnut shaft held carved images of the heads of different game that roamed the forest and hillsides surrounding them. A wolf's head was carved deeply into the uppermost part of the shaft. Each image glistened from being rubbed extensively with heated animal fat. Tied with rawhide to several grooves in the smoothed wood near the top of the shaft were three colorful feathers from a male pheasant which his father had killed only a few days earlier. Sartaya *is going to love this spear. I can't wait to present her with this gift.* Yukawe thanked his father with a loving embrace.

The next day, the three of them, Sartaya, Nakia, and Yukawe, met at the practice site. Sartaya and Nakia arrived first, so Sartaya decided to secure some of the targets. Many of them had come loose from other tribe members practicing. Some had fallen victim to night-marauding deer that had munched on the conveniently tied clumps of grass. Yukawe, carrying the new bow and arrows his father had surprised him with that very morning, finally joined them. He also carried a rolled up animal skin.

Nakia approached Yukawe, sniffing the animal skin for familiar scents. Sartaya's curiosity got the better of her, so she approached him as well. "Why did you bring the animal skin?"

"I brought something very special and it's wrapped up inside the skin," he answered. "Why don't you unwrap it for me while I help you secure the targets?" The unsuspecting girl unwrapped the well-tied deerskin to reveal the most beautiful spear she had ever seen.

She jumped back in amazement and exclaimed, "How very lucky

you are to have such an amazing spear. Did your father give this to you?"

"Yes. He made it for me because I asked him to." Sartaya asked if she could hold it and the boy nodded. It felt perfectly balanced, and it had so many beautiful carvings on it. She ran her fingers over the entire walnut shaft touching all the exquisite carvings burnt into the wood. She was so happy for Yukawe. "You must be very proud to have a spear such as this."

He smiled mischievously. "Take a closer look at the carving near the top." As she did, she began to put the symbols together in her mind. It didn't make sense at first. Then she realized what her eyes were seeing. Her wolf symbol was emblazoned into the wood.

"Yes," he said. "This spear is yours. I asked my father to make it for you. I wanted to thank you for your kindness and for helping me to discover the real reason why I wasn't successful at hunting with the bow my father made for me. Then, you invited me to hunt with you and to use your bow to get my first kill. I am so grateful to you. How do you like your new spear?"

Sartaya's eyes glistened as she looked over every detail of the spear. "Thank you, Yukawe. Thank you so very much. I can't wait to show it to my grandparents."

"My father told me he will teach you how to use and throw the spear, if you would like him to," Yukawe added. Sartaya nodded excitedly.

The three of them spent most of the afternoon at the practice range, not with their bows so much as Sartaya's new spear. When it was close to dinner time, they headed back to the campsite. As they parted toward their separate shelters, Sartaya said, "Thank you, Yukawe for such a thoughtful gift. I love it."

Wakishtay was visiting with his brother and his mate when Sartaya entered the shelter excitedly. "Look! Look at what Yukawe gave me." Of course, they already knew that Lakato had made a spear for her. "What do you think of my spear?" she asked.

"It's beautiful, Sartaya!" her grandmother exclaimed.

"Look at the carvings! Only Lakato could carve this kind of detail," Maskanini said.

"The spear point is hard and sharp and shaped just right," Wakishtay said with great admiration. Everyone took the chance to hold and admire the spear.

"It's a wonderful gift," they all said in unison. "You are a very lucky girl."

Yukawe was happy everything turned out as it had. *I have to thank my father for making such a special spear for my special friend.* As he entered his parents' shelter, Yukawe went up to Lakato and embraced him. He thanked him again for making his friend the most beautiful spear he had ever seen. Both his mother and his father beamed with pride, knowing their son was maturing and so thoughtful of others. His mother, Bosaata, asked him to untie a deerskin that was tied too tightly for her. Yukawe struggled for a few moments with the knotted rawhide before the knots finally yielded to his youthful strength. Once unstrung, the deerskin unfurled and out fell a spear.

"Ai! Yi! Yi! Yi!" he yelled.

This spear, too, was exquisitely carved with the birds and animals their tribe hunted. A male turkey was given a prominent place on the spear shaft. There were also images of pheasant, beaver, deer, elk, moose, bear, and smaller game. Lakato had also carved his son's symbol, a man chasing after a mountain lion. All of the carvings were of the entire animal, not just the heads of the animals like on Sartaya's spear. Tied to the top of the spear with rawhide were three large black and white feathers from the turkey Yukawe recently killed.

The girl known as Sartaya, and the boy known as Yukawe slept deeply that night, dreaming the dreams of young hunters with their bows secured on their shoulders and spears held tightly in their hands.

In the days that followed, the two of them were often seen together, he with his spear and she with hers. Lakato, true to his word, taught both of them how to hunt and defend themselves with their spears. They, and of course Nakia, spent a lot of time at the practice range. Lakato noticed the spears were not damaged too badly after fifteen days of training. Though, it did take a lot of patience for him to remain calm during some of the practice sessions. "After all, they are just children," he reminded himself.

CHAPTER 11

After twenty days of training, Lakato decided it was time for Yukawe and Sartaya to see how a spear was used to hunt and kill prey. After checking with the girl's grandparents, Lakato invited his son, Sartaya, and Nakia on a hunt with him. He, of course, would kill the prey with his spear to show the two young hunters how it should be done.

The morning sun peeked above the eastern horizon as the three hunters and Nakia headed out. Anxious, Miantra watched as the foursome disappeared into the forest bordering their camp. She couldn't shake the feeling this hunt was going to be different in some way. *At least, she has her wolf to protect her. Maybe I'll mention my feelings to Wakishtay after he gets up. Ah, maybe I'm just getting old. I don't want to be accused of being a worrier, yet there is this feeling deep in my stomach that something's just not right.* With that worried thought, she busied herself with her morning chores, all the time keeping a watchful eye on Wakishtay's shelter.

As the four hunters made their way into the forest, Lakato noted the beauty of the morning. The sun had painted the wispy clouds of the eastern sky with varied hues of purple, lavender, and maroon. Then a hint of orange and deep red appeared within the purples. *Breathtaking,* he thought. *I never tire of the beauty. I wonder if these two young hunters have noticed the feast of colors our Great Spirit has offered us on this glorious morning.* Thank you, he prayed silently.

Lakato felt reassured the spirits of his ancestors had blessed this day, and that this hunt would be successful. "Have you two noticed the beautiful sunrise, this morning?" They looked up toward the sky.

“Wow!” they exclaimed.

“What will we be hunting today, father?” Yukawe asked.

“Deer,” his father said. “Even though you have brought your spears with you today, I will be killing the deer so you can see the correct way of hunting live game with a spear. It will be a few more summers before either of you are ready for that.” The boy and girl looked at each other in disappointment.

Sartaya spotted the fresh tracks of several deer. “They went through here a short time ago,” she whispered. Lakato brought his fingers to his lips and motioned for everyone to remain silent. He thought the deer were close, probably grazing on the bountiful grass and plant life in the area. For his spear to be most effective, Lakato liked to be within eighteen to twenty-four paces of his prey. He had felled game from even greater distances, but not many hunters had his skill.

The hunting party suddenly stopped. Nakia sensed an animal or animals just upwind and not too far from them. He stopped and looked directly into Sartaya’s eyes. Then, Sartaya, with her keenly developed sense of smell, also recognized the scent, and signaled confirmation to Nakia. Lakato took in their interaction. *They work well together*, he observed. Yukawe didn’t make a move or sound once he saw Nakia stop.

Lakato crept forward, motioning to the others not to move. After about nine paces, he heard the rustling of tall grass as the deer fed and moved around. As he moved even closer, he made out three deer resting on the grass and turning their heads to take a mouthful of the tall, fresh-green grass nearby. Sartaya and Yukawe watched as he approached ever closer to the unsuspecting deer.

I could leap onto the male deer that is closest to me. He shouldn’t be able to get up before I thrust my spear deep into his chest, he thought. *The animal shouldn’t suffer at all.* Lakato leapt forward onto the startled buck and drove his spear deep into the animal’s side until it pierced the heart. The deer never made it to its feet. The two does jumped up and quickly bounded out of sight. Nakia waited until he received a nod from his sister before he lunged at the deer’s throat, tearing through one of its arteries. Sartaya had mentioned to Lakato, earlier, about the training ritual with Nakia after a kill. He understood and had no problem with it. Meanwhile, he was having trouble pulling his spear out of the deer.

As both Yukawe and Sartaya approached the kill, a deep-bellied growl came from behind them. They both turned. No more than forty-five paces downwind from them crouched a large mountain lion. It must have picked up their scent several miles back as they were tracking the deer. It was probably thinking that either one of these young defenseless humans would be an easier kill then trying to snatch the downed deer from the hunter and the wolf. It would also be easier to carry the smaller human than the large deer to its den.

Nakia, gorging himself with the deer's blood and some raw flesh from its neck area, looked up when he heard a strange animal's growl followed by Sartaya's and Yukawe's scream of alarm.

* * *

Back at the tribal camp, about mid-morning, Miantra found the old hunter stirring about outside his shelter. Wakishtay was still trying to get the sleep dust out of his eyes when the mate of his brother approached him.

"Brother to my mate, I'm worried about Sartaya."

"What worries you so early in the day?" he asked. Miantra told him her feelings about this special hunt that Sartaya and her friend, Yukawe, had went on with Lakato.

"Please don't think that I'm just some old woman who worries about everything, because I'm not. I never worried nor did I feel like this when you and Sartaya went hunting. I know Lakato is a great hunter and can take care of himself, so I don't know why I feel this way." Wakishtay stopped what he was doing and gathered-up his bow and arrows. He trusted this woman's instincts.

"Which way did they head out of camp?" He tried not to alarm her even more than she already was.

Wakishtay picked up the trail left by the three humans and the wolf. Then the trail cooled off somewhat and he had no idea how far they had already gone. Nor did he know what he would say to Lakato once he caught up to them. The old hunter certainly had no intention of embarrassing him, especially in front of the children. He had much respect for this man who had made his granddaughter that splendid spear. He did quicken his steps, though.

* * *

In the blink of an eye, Sartaya and Yukawe remembered what Lakato had taught them about defending themselves with a spear against larger animals. They fell to their knees, braced the butt of their spears into the ground between their legs, and pointed their spears toward the onrushing mountain lion. Nakia, understanding the danger approaching his human sister, howled fiercely as he sprang toward the two young hunters. Unfortunately, he was too many steps away to get between them and the attacking cat before it reached them.

Lakato yanked on his spear. *Why won't it come loose? Great Spirit, please help me free my spear!* In that moment, he pulled his spear loose from the deer's side. Then he twisted around to throw his spear with all of his strength toward the leaping cat, but it was too late. He ran toward the cat and the two children, hoping for the best, but fearing the worst.

Distracted by Nakia's fierce howl, the cat made a fatal mistake and leapt between the girl and the boy. The space separating them was minimal. The cat didn't see the two spear points aimed at its chest and belly until it was too late. The cat twisted its body in vain. The mountain lion's full weight buried the spear points deep within its body and it fell, dead, on top of the two young hunters.

Nakia lunged toward its neck, severing an artery that no longer carried the life sustaining blood from its heart.

Lakato couldn't believe what he had just witnessed. These two children, no, these two young hunters had kept their wits about them in the face of certain death . . . and triumphed. Lakato couldn't have been more proud of his son and the young girl by his side. With spear in hand, he walked over to where the two were lying with the mountain lion on top of them, nearly hiding them from sight.

"How long are you two planning to just lie around? Come on, there is work to be done," he chided. He pulled the dead mountain lion off of them. Nakia's jaws were still locked on the cat's neck.

Sartaya motioned for him to back off, and he did so, reluctantly. "A mountain lion, a deer, three bloody spears, a wolf with a red snout, and two very lucky young hunters. Who will ever believe this story?" he wondered out-loud.

"I will," shouted Wakishtay as he approached the bloody scene. "I saw the mountain lion just as it leapt for your son and my granddaughter. I didn't see their spears. I thought these two would be killed for sure. Then I saw Nakia lunging for the cat's throat and I thought for a brief moment that just maybe it wouldn't be as bad as I feared. Then, these two young hunters saved their own lives." He glanced down at Yukawe and Sartaya. "What do you think, Lakato? Should we help them gut their kill?"

"Yes, Wakishtay, they should be the ones who gut this animal. Besides, there will be much excitement in the camp over this kill. They might as well get the credit and admiration for cleaning their kill too."

It took some time because Sartaya and Yukawe wanted to do the entire gutting of the mountain lion themselves. The two men guided the young hunters' hands, then stood back to watch them complete the bloody but necessary work. Much pride filled the two grown men's hearts. Once the task was finished, Wakishtay cut out the heart of the mountain lion and placed it in a skin bag he always carried with him on hunting trips. Nakia was given the heart of the deer which he truly enjoyed. Lakato found a handful of dead branches large enough to carry the two dead animals. One end of a pair of poles would be lifted onto one of the shoulders of each hunter where they could then grip them, while the other ends of the poles would drag on the ground. The two men would drag one pair of poles that had the deer tied across them, while Yukawe and Sartaya carried the mountain lion on the second pair.

The hunting party finally arrived at camp close to dinner time. Although the mountain lion was a heavy load for these two youngsters to carry, once everyone saw them and cheers and yelling filled their ears, the load seemed much lighter.

A few dozen steps inside the camp's perimeter, a handful of strong young braves rushed out to carry both kills to the center of the encampment. Excitement swelled around the four hunters as curiosity rose about the mountain lion. Wakishtay raised his hands to quiet the excited group of children and adults. “It is time for four very hungry hunters to have dinner. Tonight, when the sun is low and the campfire roars, Lakato and I will share with all of you the story of how these two young hunters killed this mountain lion.”

Miantra, who had heard what happened, waited until Sartaya came into their shelter before she held out her arms to welcome her granddaughter safely home. The young girl dropped her spear and ran into her grandmother’s waiting arms. “Oh Grandmother, I was so afraid I was going to die!” Tears flowed down her dusty cheeks while she sobbed. Miantra, whose cheeks were moist from tears of joy, gently stroked her granddaughter’s hair, not being able to imagine what the girl had just been through.

“You’re home and you’re safe now,” she whispered. “Were you hurt? You’re covered with blood.”

“No, just scared,” Sartaya said. “The blood belongs to the mountain lion.”

“Sartaya, I love you very much and I am so glad you came home safe and unhurt.”

“ME TOO, Grandmother, ME TOO!”

CHAPTER 12

Excitement filled the air as everyone hurried through their evening meal, wishing the tribal campfire would somehow come sooner. It seemed to take forever before several men finally built the campfire up to where they wanted it. But before the fire was blazing, most families had already taken seats around it. No one wanted to miss any of the spectacular story about the mountain lion and the two young hunters.

Finally, Lakato and his family, followed by Wakishtay, Nakia, Maskanini and his family arrived and seated themselves. Next to them, KiaNeeishtay, smiling broadly, faced his people. The mountain lion's hide, with its head still attached and jaws propped wide-open showing off its huge fangs, was placed on a stick-rack and propped up seven paces from the ground behind the two young hunters.

"Tonight is very special for us all. We have before us, two young hunters and one very large mountain lion. Are we supposed to believe these two young hunters killed this lion?" KiaNeeishtay said as he smiled warmly at Sartaya and Yukawe. "Maybe Lakato and Wakishtay can tell the rest of us what really happened? It should make for a good story, don't you think?" Everyone cheered in agreement. With that, the tribal leader sat down among Yukawe, Sartaya, and their families.

Lakato spoke first. He told everyone exactly what happened up to when the lion came into view of Yukawe and Sartaya. Then Lakato sat down and Wakishtay stood and related what had happened earlier that day according to his recollection. He stopped at the point where he first saw the mountain lion. Then, he looked at the two young hunters with much affection and pride and motioned for them to take his place in front of the tribe and continue with the rest of the story.

The two young hunters looked at each other anxiously and slowly stood up. Their clothes were still stained with the mountain lion's blood. They were very embarrassed to take the storyteller's place. Usually, children were not asked to actively participate in Story Telling. Instead, they were expected to observe and learn from the stories told by the adults.

Sartaya nodded to Yukawe and her eyes pleaded with him to begin. He reluctantly returned her nod and faced the Nataych tribal members. At first he couldn't speak, but then with an encouraging look from his father, he began. Fortunately, he had brought his spear, as had Sartaya. Everyone was on the edge of their rock or log-stump seats, not wanting to miss one word these young and courageous children had to say.

"We were watching my father kill the deer when we heard a loud growl behind us. We both turned to see this large mountain lion getting ready to attack us. Before then, we had no idea it had been tracking us. Sartaya and I saw the terror in each other's eyes. We had no time to say anything. But we both knew what to do as the huge cat leapt toward us. We buried the end of our spear shafts into the ground like this, just as my father had trained us, and pointed our spears directly at the lunging mountain lion. We got as close to the ground as we could, closed our eyes, and screamed as the cat leapt."

Yukawe then nodded to Sartaya to continue with the story. "I remember hearing another ferocious growling and barking as Nakia lunged at the cat from where the deer was laying. Then the mountain lion plunged onto our spears and knocked us over. Our spears killed the lion, but we couldn't move with the weight of the huge cat on top of us. Lakato finally lifted the dead lion off and said, 'How long are you two planning to just lie around? Come on, there is work to be done.'" The entire tribe broke into laughter.

The tribal leader stood up and laid his hands on the shoulders of the two youngsters. "These two young hunters were very brave and will be honored at a special ceremonial campfire in two days. Since most of you have never tasted the meat from a mountain lion, you will all be given an opportunity to try some of the meat at the ceremony. Everyone is to bring food for this celebration. Lakato's mate, Bosaata, will get with each of you in preparation for this ceremonial banquet." After he gestured that the campfire was over, everyone jumped up and clapped and yelled their approval. Everyone wanted to get a closer look at the lion and tell the two young hunters how proud they were of them. Finally, after satisfying everyone's curiosity, the two returned to their shelters for a well-deserved night's sleep.

CHAPTER 13

During the next two days, excitement over the ceremony that would take place filled everyone in the tribe. Bosaata met with each of the women to discuss the food that would be served at the ceremonial banquet. She wasn't surprised that the women had never prepared or tasted mountain lion meat. They decided preparing it the same way they prepared deer meat would suffice.

For the better part of a day, the tribal leader, Maskanini, Miantra, Wakishtay, and Lakato huddled together in KiaNeeishtay's shelter. They were planning a very special ceremony to honor Sartaya, Yukawe, and the tribe's good fortune of having killed a rogue mountain lion.

In the meantime, Sartaya and Yukawe entertained the other children and many adults with their enactment of the attack and their incredible feat of killing the mountain lion. They never seemed to tire of telling their story at the least amount of encouragement.

On the day of the ceremony, excitement and the delicious aromas from all the prepared food filled the air. Everyone gathered in a circle around the makeshift branch and rock structures on which all of the food was placed. KiaNeeishtay motioned for everyone's attention and then nodded to Maskanini. Maskanini raised his hands toward their ancestors looming high in the sky above them.

"Great Spirit, we give thanks to you for our good fortune. We are honored that you and so many of our ancestors have joined us for this very special and unusual ceremony. Never before, in the memories of our elders, has there been a killing of a mountain lion by two children. It is so rare for such a great animal to even wander this close to a camp or be seen by our hunters."

He continued, "We will try to explain what is meant by this mountain lion coming into our lives, especially the lives of these two young and very brave children. But first, we will enjoy this feast that has been prepared for us. Everyone should taste the meat of the mountain lion, for it will give strength to your spirit. Sartaya and Yukawe will have the honor to be first in line. Just as we have always honored our hunters upon returning with their kills, these two will receive the choicest pieces of the mountain lion's meat." This was by far the greatest feast of the Natayeh in recent memory, and the ceremony afterwards promised to be every bit as exciting.

Sartaya and Yukawe were embarrassed to be the guests of honor and first in line before even the tribe's leader. KiaNeeishtay, however, placed his hands on their shoulders, and his smiling eyes put them both at ease. "I will show you the choicest pieces of the lion's meat. Here, take these two chunks that have been cut just for you. I am very proud of the courage that you both displayed in the face of certain death. You have brought great honor to the Natayeh People. Now, help yourself to the rest of the food prepared with great care by the women of our tribe. Then, come and sit by me to eat. I want to hear all about your last two days."

Sartaya's grandparents, Wakishtay, Maskanini and Miantra, as well as Yukawe's parents, Lakato and Bosaata joined the two children in a small circle with the Tribal Leader and his mate, Miikwasi. The adults enjoyed watching and listening to the two brave children explaining and acting out, in between mouthfuls of delicious food, the excitement of their last two days.

There was plenty of food left over once everyone had their fill. The women parceled out the remnants of the feast to each person who quickly tucked them into their shelter's underground storage so they could return to the campfire. No one wanted to miss what came next.

CHAPTER 14

The last glimmer of the sun's crimson red and orange rays disappeared below the western horizon. The night sky glittered with the spirits of all the ancestors who had come to watch over this ceremony. As the campfire burned lower and the moon shone brightly, everyone found a comfortable place on the ground around the fire pit to sit. The two guests of honor sat in front of the tribal leader. Sartaya's grandparents and Yukawe's parents sat on opposite sides of the leader. Only the crackling of the dying campfire broke the silence. KiaNeeishtay rose and raised his hands to call upon the ancestral spirits for their approval of this night's special ceremony.

"You have all heard, by now, the story of how a mountain lion attacked these two children of the Natayeh. Yet, these two children, Sartaya and Yukawe, defended themselves and killed this powerful animal. You may have asked yourselves, 'How could this be?' I know that I have. I also know their parents and grandparents are bewildered as to how these two children could have survived this mountain lion attack. It just doesn't seem possible. But here we are, celebrating their lives and the death of the mountain lion. What could all of this possibly mean?

"With the help of our Ancestral Spirits we will try to understand. For now, we call upon Miantra, who can speak with and understand animals, to help us." KiaNeeishtay motioned for her to rise.

She stood beside the two children. "A mountain lion is the fastest and most powerful of the animals that roam our hunting grounds. It is a smart and stealthy hunter whose favorite prey is the deer which are abundant throughout our forests. The mountain lion can teach us how to bring out the courage and strength within each of us. It can fill our hearts with this courage and strength so we can defend ourselves, or attack with equal effectiveness. Every one of us can benefit from this experience in some way. However, we must remember that the mountain lion attacked these two children sitting beside me. It intended to kill them, but then, incredibly, it was killed instead by these very same children."

Miantra turned toward the two children and continued. "I believe that this mountain lion came into both of your lives to help you to survive even greater challenges that have yet to make themselves known to you. Chanutey—*Mountain Lion's Spirit*, was asked to sacrifice itself by the Great Spirit so that you may survive these unknown challenges. This was truly a great and powerful mountain lion for it to be asked by the Great Spirit to die for you. We will call it Lion Spirit and it will be honored by our ancestors forevermore. There will be a very special place in the night sky for this kindred spirit." Having said that, Miantra smiled lovingly at the two children, then sat down.

Maskanini stood up and asked the two children to stand on either side of him. "A mountain lion's claws can kill another animal quickly and efficiently. The claws also defend the mountain lion against all attackers. Because it is not known what great challenges may lie ahead for you, it is only fitting that we honor you both with the claws from this powerful animal. By wearing these claws around your neck, all others will be reminded of your tremendous bravery and courage. The spirit of this mountain lion will give you the necessary strength and power needed to face your future challenges." Yukawe and Sartaya accepted their lion-claw necklaces with true humility as Maskanini placed one over each of their heads. The tribe cheered loudly.

Maskanini then motioned for Wakishtay to come forward. Wakishtay held a bowl of cooked meat chunks. He asked Sartaya and Yukawe to take a piece and eat it. They did. "This is the heart of the mountain lion that attacked you and that you, then, killed. By eating its heart you will always have the strength and courage of this ferocious animal's spirit in your own heart and spirit. Remember this day, for the time will come when you will need to draw upon this same strength and courage to survive your greatest challenges."

As Wakishtay was about to give the remaining chunks of meat to the hunters of the tribe, Sartaya grabbed his hand. "Grandfather, could you give the rest of the mountain lion's heart to the other children so they can become strong and courageous when they face their greatest challenges? The hunters are already strong and courageous. Don't the children need it more?"

Those closest smiled in amazement at her wisdom and nodded their approval. Wakishtay too was surprised at her words. *I cannot help but wonder if this girl is not destined for greatness.*

"I invite all the children to please come forward to taste the heart of the mountain lion so that your spirits will be filled with strength and courage when you face your greatest challenges." The children felt honored to be included in this wonderful ceremony. There will be many exciting dreams tonight, he thought to himself. The old hunter nodded to Lakato as he sat down. The rest of the tribe, especially the elders, took special note of Sartaya's thoughtfulness and wisdom.

Lakato could not have been more proud of his son and, of course, Sartaya. He stood up and spoke. "When I saw this ferocious mountain lion leaping through the air toward these two children, with its fangs bared and claws outstretched, I was sure they would both be killed. The spears that I made for them, plus their quick thinking, and their courage in the face of certain death, saved their lives. It would only be fitting for their spears to now have a mountain lion carved into them." The rest of the tribe shouted their agreement. Lakato turned to his mate, Bosaata, who handed him the two spears. He, in turn, handed the spears to Sartaya and Yukawe. Each shaft now had, in addition to the figures that were originally carved into them, a magnificent carving of a mountain lion with a spear buried in its chest. Sartaya and Yukawe reached excitedly for their spears, and then, with glistening eyes, hugged Lakato. The entire Tribe rose and cheered.

Over the next sixteen days, the bones from the mountain lion were dried and blanched by the sun. Wakishtay and Lakato gave bone fragments from the Lion to each man, woman, and child. This gift was held in high esteem by everyone. Some members bored holes in the fragments and strung them onto their Life's Necklace along with other meaningful bones, stones, and shells. Others did the same, only with bracelets. The two men safely stored the remaining bones for a future event they had in mind. The creature's skull, with jaw open and fangs bared, was placed on top of a branch pole next to the Tribe's main campfire pit for all to see.

It took Wakishtay one full moon of effort before he presented Lakato with the cured hide of the mountain lion. Lakato, appreciative and grateful to Wakishtay for his thoughtfulness, gave the hide to his son who was overjoyed and promised to cherish it for all time. Yukawe used it as his sleeping hide every night thereafter. Many nights, while curled up in the beautiful soft hide of the mountain lion, Yukawe had strange and exciting dreams that included the mountain lion's spirit watching over and protecting him from harm.

CHAPTER 15

Even though three full moons had passed, the mountain lion attack on Sartaya and Yukawe was still very fresh in the minds of most people. It was especially raw in Miantra's heart because she had nearly lost her precious granddaughter. Miantra decided that, for awhile at least, Sartaya needed to spend time learning the other skills needed to survive, and less time developing her hunting and tracking skills.

Miantra received no arguments from the men in her life—Maskanini and Wakishtay. Even Sartaya thought she would enjoy learning more about gathering vegetables and herbs for cooking and medicines, the making of clothes and jewelry, as well as what it took to make a shelter. She understood females needed to learn these things and be able to do them by their thirteenth summer. These skills were in addition to their child bearing and nurturing responsibilities. Though, Natayeh women were also encouraged to learn how to catch fish and to track and hunt animals if they desired or had to under special circumstances.

The men were expected to know something of the same skills that women learned, though their primary responsibilities were tracking, hunting, and fishing. They also had to be proficient in making canoes, weapons such as bows and arrows, spears, and knives, and in setting traps. This separation of key responsibilities and blending of skills among the men and women of the Natayeh had brought balance and harmony to their lives for many generations.

Sartaya knew Nakia would quickly tire of looking for plants with her or sitting by her side while she sewed clothes or footwear. She went to Wakishtay and asked, "Would you take Nakia with you when you go tracking and hunting for awhile? Over the next few moons, Miantra wants me to learn as much as I can about roots and plants and medicines. Nakia won't understand why I'm not tracking or hunting and he would get bored with what I am doing. It would mean so much to me to know he's with you."

"I will be happy to take your brother with me. I think I'll also ask Yukawe to come with us. He still has much to learn about tracking and hunting." The old hunter motioned to Nakia to walk by his side. The wolf trotted happily as they headed over to Lakato's shelter.

Yukawe looked at his father for his approval. Lakato smiled and nodded. Excited, Yukawe gathered his bow and quiver of arrows, leaving his spear behind.

On the way out of camp, Nakia stole a quick glance at his sister. She waved goodbye as they disappeared into the edge of the forest. *I really wish I was going with them. I hope there are no more mountain lions nearby,* she thought with dread.

Sartaya helped Miantra finish her morning chores. Over the last several summers the old woman had taught her granddaughter how to find and gather most food plants, and how to prepare them. *Now it's time for Sartaya to learn about the medicinal plants Maskanini and I use.* Miantra decided to start the lessons with a very special root and its healing characteristics.

She reached out for the young girl's hand. Sartaya eagerly clasped it as they walked toward the edge of camp swinging their arms back and forth. The old woman smiled as the child in her heart returned. *It will be nice to be with my granddaughter, just the two of us.*

"We don't have to travel very far to find this special plant. It helps calm coughs and quiet the rattling in your chest." They had not walked very far when Miantra stopped and pointed to a patch of leaves and tiny flowers clinging to the forest floor. "We call this plant the Coughing Root. Remember where we found it and what the leaves and flowers look like. We'll take some of the plant and its roots back to camp. We must be careful not to damage the rest of the plant when we dig some up. That way it will keep growing and always be here when we need it."

After digging up several clumps of Coughing Root, they headed back to camp. Sartaya daydreamed about Nakia and wondered what kind of adventures he and her grandfather were getting into. *Nakia would not have had fun with me today.*

When she and her grandmother returned to camp, the older woman started a small fire in their shelter. "Sartaya, will you take these plants and rinse them in the stream to get all the dirt off? Take this bowl with you and fill it halfway with fresh water." Miantra smiled at her granddaughter as she handed her the empty bowl. *There is so much to teach her. I wonder if she will take to it. At least she is not being chased by hungry mountain lions while with me.*

Sartaya returned with the clean plants and half-full bowl of water. "Now what do we do, Grandmother?"

Miantra showed her how to mash the roots with a specially designed stone tool. After the roots were mashed they placed them into the heated water. Once the water started boiling, Miantra poured some of the hot liquid into a smaller bowl. They both tasted the hot liquid. "It's not at all bitter like I thought it would be, Grandmother. It does have a unique flavor, though."

"Slowly sipping this boiled root broth usually helps to reduce chronic coughing," Miantra said. "Now we will place the leaves and roots on the fire. As they begin to smolder, breathe in their smoke." As they did, Sartaya began to choke and cough. "Try not to breathe in the smoke too quickly. Let it gather around you, then using your hands gently push some of it towards your nose and mouth. Breathe it in slowly, but not to the point of choking. This will help to still the rattle in your throat and clear your nose when you are having difficulty breathing."

"I seem to remember the smell of the smoke, Grandmother. Is this what you gave me five winters ago when my chest felt heavy and I was having so much trouble breathing?"

"Yes. That's why I chose to teach you about this plant today." They both smiled at each other as they remembered. "This plant helped to clear your nose and lungs and improve your breathing. It's been used for this purpose for a very long time by our ancestors and now by us. My mother taught me how to use it just as her mother had taught her.

"The root can also be mashed and applied to skin rashes and sore muscles that surround our knees, wrists, elbows, fingers, and toes. There are other plants that can treat these conditions. Sometimes, we have to try different plants until we find one that works well for the person being treated. We may have to combine several medicinal plants in order to provide relief. And sometimes, nothing works and we feel badly that we couldn't help the person. But we must never stop trying to help, because just trying makes a big difference in how they feel and how quickly they get better. It's as though their spirits appreciate the effort we are making and want to help us heal them more quickly. I don't know how or why it happens this way, but I do know that it does. I have seen it myself, many times."

The old woman smiled. "We are finished for today, Sartaya. You can join your friends for the rest of the day. Tomorrow, I will help you discover another important plant that can be very useful in helping people to sleep."

"Thank you, Grandmother, for teaching me about the Coughing Root. Did your mother teach you all that you know about plant medicines?"

"She taught me much, but my grandmother also taught me a lot. I never told you this before but, throughout the ages, all of my ancestors were medicine women. These same medicine women are your ancestors, too. Perhaps, one day their spirits will talk to you as they have talked to me."

"What do you mean, Grandmother? What did they say to you?"

"Go now and be with your friends. We'll talk more about this another day."

I'm really curious about what grandmother meant about my ancestors talking to me, Sartaya thought. They hugged each other, and then Sartaya left to find her friends.

CHAPTER 16

Sartaya had been playing with her friends for most of the afternoon when she spotted Nakia, Yukawe, and her grandfather returning from their day's adventure. Nakia looked up to the old man for permission to run to his sister. After a slight nod from Wakishtay, Nakia bounded over to Sartaya. The three hunters had missed her company that day. Wakishtay especially missed having his granddaughter by his side. *I know it's for the best. She must learn what Miantra has to teach her. There will be other days for us to be together. And Nakia and Yukawe were good companions today.*

Nakia, now fully grown, had to be careful not to knock his sister down when she bent over to put her arms around him. "Nakia, I missed you today. Did you have fun with Grandfather and Yukawe?" Nakia's tail wagged as he licked her cheek.

Wakishtay carried a colorful male pheasant Yukawe had shot with an arrow. The wolf's face was red with blood from attacking the pheasant's throat. Sartaya laughed at him. The children she had been playing with had followed her and now surrounded the three hunters. They wanted to see what the hunters had killed. Yukawe enjoyed their attention. There was also a good chance Yukawe and Sartaya would see that each one of them received at least one of the bird's feathers. The children always prized these small, thoughtful gifts whenever Sartaya, Yukawe, and her grandfather returned from a successful hunt.

Nakia spent most of the next day with the old hunter and Yukawe while they repaired the practice shooting area now being used by the entire tribe. The grass mock-up figures that resembled different animals needed a lot of attention. Many deer also frequented the practice range. They preferred munching late in the evening on the tied bundles of long grass that resembled various animals. The old hunter suspected they thought these bundles were placed there just for them. *One of these days when the tribe needs more meat I'm going to hide near the practice area late in the evening and wait for some of these four-legged marauders. Then . . . .*

CHAPTER 17

Sartaya and her grandmother went on another of their learning and teaching trips. This day Miantra planned to show her granddaughter how to identify the Sleeping Plant and where to find it. It took them more time than expected to find this most useful plant. Once they did, they again carefully dug up some of the plant's roots and gathered some of its leafy branches before returning to camp. "Grandmother, is this plant only used to make medicine that helps us sleep?"

"It has several other uses. Let's head down to the stream and I'll help you to rinse these plants off."

"You don't have to help me, Grandmother. I can do it by myself."

"I know you can. I just want to walk with you. It makes me happy to be near you." They both smiled at each other.

"I love you too, Grandmother."

After they returned to camp Miantra built a small fire for boiling water. "I'll run down to the stream and fill this bowl with fresh water," Sartaya said.

"Thank you, Sartaya. While you're doing that, I'll separate the leaves from the branches and begin crushing these roots."

"Oh. I like to do that too. Save some for me to crush." It didn't take Sartaya very long to run down to the fast running stream for fresh water, then return to her shelter.

"Place the bowl by the fire on this hot stone," Miantra said. "I left most of the roots for you. Here, use this stone. As you crush them, drain the fluid into this smaller bowl. It may take some time because you have to be very careful to get as much of the liquid from the crushed roots as possible into the bowl. That's it. We're not in any hurry. You're doing very well, Sartaya."

After a short time Sartaya said, "I don't think there is any more juice to mash out of these roots, Grandmother."

"Good. We have enough to give to Wakishtay tonight to help him sleep. His bones are very old. His body cries out in pain every day."

"Is that why Maskanini always gives him a pouch of medicine every night? Does it help him to sleep?"

"Yes. Wakishtay has always been the greatest hunter of our tribe, but his body is tired and worn out. He provided meat for this tribe when no other hunters could. All the summers of tracking, hunting, and carrying his kills back to camp have taken a toll on his body. During some of the most severe winters, it was only his skills that provided us with meat. We are all grateful for what he has done for us."

"He usually doesn't get a liquid from Maskanini," Sartaya said.

"No, Maskanini usually gives him one of these roots to chew on until he feels drowsy enough to fall asleep. But the liquid from this plant is stronger than just chewing on the root for some of its juices. He will sleep throughout the night and probably won't awaken until late morning. After spending most of the day with Nakia and Yukawe repairing the practice shooting area, he will be tired and his body will be very sore. The long rest will help soothe the pain. Tomorrow, you, Nakia, and Yukawe can spend the entire day with your grandfather."

"Oh, thank you, Grandmother! I really missed being with them the last two days. Aren't we going to boil these crushed roots?"

"No. The boiling water is for a soothing and relaxing hot drink for you and me. Before I pour you a cup . . . ."

"What about the leaves and what's left of the roots from the Sleeping Plant? What are we going to do with them?"

"Be patient, Sartaya. Now, the crushed root can be applied directly to an injured area to help reduce the pain from a wound or bruise. We can also dry the crushed roots, then crush them into a powder. The powder can then be spread onto an open wound to help keep it clean and quicken the healing process."

"What about the plant's leaves?"

"I want you to roll them up with your fingers and squeeze them until they bruise. That's it. Now drop them into the boiling water. We'll also add some roots from the Quiet Tree to the water. I've shown you before where to find this tree and what it is used for. Remember?"

"Yes, I remember how it tasted and how it made me feel calm. Why are we adding leaves from the Sleeping Plant?"

"Now stir the roots and the leaves until the water turns color." After stirring it, the hot liquid began to turn a light greenish brown. "It's ready to drink." Miantra poured the liquid into two small drinking bowls. "By adding the leaves from the Sleeping Plant, the hot water now has a unique flavor. Come sit on my lap. This drink will calm us and relax us. Let's just sip it for awhile."

Sartaya felt very comfortable cradled in her grandmother's arms. She treasured these moments of intimacy. After just a few sips of the liquid, her eyelids became heavy. "If you want to close your eyes, then do so." Miantra, also feeling the effects of the relaxing hot drink, closed her eyes. Both of them were in a dreamlike state; completely relaxed and open for what was about to happen. With their eyes closed, they might have appeared to be asleep. But their spirits were awakened and actively engaged in conversation.

"Grandmother, this is such a strange feeling. We're not talking, yet I can hear you. Our eyes are closed but I can see you. Who are these other people? I've never seen any of them before but part of me seems to know who they are. I'm confused."

"Your eyes have never seen them before, but your spirit knows them well. They are your ancestors. They were medicine men and medicine women of our tribe. They have been waiting patiently through the ages for you to be born, and then for you to become old enough to learn what they have to teach you. Listen carefully to them and learn from them, just as I have throughout most of my life."

"But why do they want me, Grandmother?" The answer came, but not from her grandmother.

"Sartaya, our spirits are joining together with yours. Don't be afraid. We have waited until your spirit was of age to understand what we are about to teach you. From the beginning of our people's time there have been medicine men and medicine women. The very first medicine woman was taught by a very powerful Maskanini who took her for his mate. He taught her everything he knew about the many uses of plants, roots, and trees and how they can be used as medicine to help care for their people. They became even more knowledgeable about these things as they grew older together. But they both died unexpectedly without passing any of this knowledge on."

Her ancient ancestors continued, "Not wanting their knowledge to be lost, their spirits made a promise to one another that from time-to-time they would pass this knowledge of medicines on to other living people. Much like what we are doing with you today, these ancient spirits chose very special people throughout the ages who had generous hearts and strong, courageous spirits. The ancients then instilled their combined knowledge of everything they knew about medicines and how these medicines should be used, into the spirits of these special people. Throughout all of time, our tribes have always depended upon these medicine men and medicine women to help them whenever anyone was sick or injured.

"We have spoken often to the spirits of your Grandfather Maskanini, and to your Grandmother Miantra. We have shared all of our knowledge with them throughout most of their lives. Recently, their spirits have reached out to us. They suggested that because they are in the late winter of their lives, we should consider helping them to pass our combined knowledge of medicine and healing to you. They know you have a generous heart and a strong, courageous spirit. They have decided you are ready and that you would make a wonderful medicine woman. We agreed. Now is the time for us to share with your spirit all that we have learned, just as we have done with your grandmother and grandfather, and their ancestors before them throughout all of time."

"Grandmother, is this really happening?"

"Yes, Sartaya, it is really happening. Now you must listen and watch with your spirit's ears and eyes."

As Sartaya's physical body rested comfortably on her grandmother's lap, the spirit of the young girl was surrounded by the spirits of all the medicine men and medicine women throughout the ages. These spirits were above her, below her, and all around her. It seemed as though they were all speaking at the same time but using different tongues. It was a cacophony of sounds. In addition to their voices, images of what they were describing flashed around each of their spirits. Time as she knew it had no meaning in this place.

Then, as abruptly as it started, it ended. One voice spoke. "Sartaya, you have been entrusted with these great and special gifts. These gifts of knowledge, of all the medicines known throughout time, come with a great responsibility. Much will be expected from you throughout your life. Your strong, courageous spirit and your generous heart will help you through the many challenges that lie ahead of you. We will also be there for you just as we have been there for your grandmother and grandfather. We must go for now. Goodbye, Sartaya, Medicine Woman."

Sartaya's eyelids fluttered as she awoke from her dreamlike state. Miantra, already awake, waited patiently for her granddaughter to rouse. "Grandmother, was I dreaming? Did all of this really happen? It all seemed so real, but how could it be?"

"Sartaya, I'm so proud of you. Yes, Granddaughter. It all really happened just as you remember it. I was only a few summers older than you when these same spirits came to me. But still, it's a lot to take in all at once and understand, no matter how old you are. Over time, you'll make sense of it all. Just know that your spirit has this tremendous amount of knowledge about healing medicines, how and when to use them, and where to find them. When the time comes, you won't have to worry about what to do. It will come naturally to you, through Spirit Whispers."

"How can I be a medicine woman like you? I'm only eleven summers old."

"I was just thirteen summers old when they came to my dreams. I never questioned their wisdom and neither should you, Sartaya. You have to believe they have a good reason for their choice of timing."

"Grandmother, there was a much older woman's spirit there and she was leaning on a crooked walking stick. It seemed like all the other spirits surrounded her and held her in the highest regard. Do you know who she was?"

"She is known as Wanastabi. Shall I tell you about her?"

“Oh, yes. I want to know everything about her. It seemed as though she never took her eyes off of me.”

Miantra smiled at her granddaughter and began her story. “The very first people to inhabit Mother Earth were called the Wijomine. The Wijomine Tribe faced many hardships we cannot imagine, but Mother Earth filled their spirits with courage and strength so they could survive.

“Throughout more Summers of Life than we can count, their numbers grew into many tribes. These tribes spread across great distances of land, snow, and water. Some eventually traveled across Ice Bridges to finally settle in the forests where we now live. After being away from their homeland for so long, these First People grew extremely homesick.

“A young girl of these very first people was known for her ability to talk with animals, snakes, and birds. One day, when she was nearly eight summers old, she broke her right leg while scampering down a rather steep hill; one she had traveled over many times before. Although her people were used to setting broken limbs, this break was particularly difficult and never healed correctly. Because of her injured leg, she had great difficulty keeping up with the constant traveling of her Wijomine Tribe, often slowing them down. But they would never leave one of their own behind, not even if it threatened their existence. Life, all life, was revered by the Wijomine.

“This girl was very strong-willed and determined not to become a burden to her people. Shortly after her fall, while hobbling across some rugged terrain, she spotted an unusual looking stick caught between several large jagged pieces of rock. She motioned to several of her older tribesmen to help her extract the odd looking stick from its rocky resting place. She beamed with joy at her newfound treasure. One of the older tribesmen recognized the wood grain as belonging to a walnut tree, which grew abundantly in the Wijomine’s homeland, many seasons travel to the Northeast of where they were at the time.

“As each member of the Wijomine Tribe inspected the newfound stick they felt something very familiar in their hearts. The oldest of the Wijomine said they were all feeling their beloved homeland. Now, they had been traveling for a very long time and missed their homeland very much. This stick was an unusual find in this region of their travels. All of them agreed it was placed in their path by Mother Earth. That very night, the Wijomine Tribe celebrated their good fortune by honoring the girl who had found this special stick. From that night forward, she was to be known as Wanastabi, Keeper of the Sacred Walking Stick.

"Throughout her life, she and the Sacred Stick from a walnut tree were inseparable. She depended on this Stick to compensate for her bad leg while traveling. Aside from helping her walk, this Sacred Stick possessed very special qualities which enabled it to absorb the lifetime memories of these First People. The Stick was always close by and available to all members of the Wijomine Tribe who, from time to time, needed to fill their hearts with the spirit and memories of their homeland. Wanastabi always felt honored to be the Keeper of such strong medicine. She enjoyed it when others came to her whenever that special place in their hearts needed to be filled again. She, along with her Sacred Stick, comforted their hearts in a way no other could.

"Her abilities combined with that of the Sacred Stick soon became well known among the various other tribes that originated from these First People. The other tribes often went out of their way to ensure their paths would cross with hers, especially if they had been away from their homeland for any significant period of time. As the seasons merged together, Wanastabi realized that instead of being a burden to her people in all the time since she'd injured her leg, she was the spiritual core that held them together.

"During the winter of her life, she returned to her homeland and gathered as many walking sticks as she could from the walnut trees that grew abundantly there. She asked Mother Earth to make them as special as her Sacred Stick so she could give one to each of the tribes that originated from the Wijomine. It was quite a task, but with the help of many she was able to complete it before her spirit rose to shine brightly in the night skies above them.

"Ever since, each of the tribes has honored and named one of their member's the Keeper of the Sacred Walking Stick. When I became a medicine woman, I was thirteen summers old. At that age, the

Natayeh also honored me by naming me the Keeper of our tribe's Sacred Walking Stick, just as my mother, and her mother before her, were honored as Keepers. Soon, Sartaya, you too will be honored to become the Keeper of our tribe's Sacred Walking Stick."

"Grandmother, why haven't I seen people coming to you and asking to hold the stick?"

"Most of the time you haven't been around when they approached me. I know you've seen me carrying the Sacred Walking Stick many times. But, you didn't think anything more about it. You were too busy playing with the other children or on your way with Wakishtay and Nakia to go hunting. You probably thought that my bones were sore and I needed it to help me walk more easily. Sometimes, that was the reason. But most of the time I was visiting with someone who had asked me if they could hold the Sacred Walking Stick because they or their family needed to fill an emptiness in their hearts.

"Bring the Sacred Walking Stick to me, Sartaya. Now sit across from me and we'll both hold onto it. There, just like that. Close your eyes and tell me what your heart sees and feels."

"Grandmother, I suddenly feel strangely wonderful. I can remember all the things that happened to me while I was growing up. I can feel all the love that you and my grandfathers had for me then, as well as now. Is this how the Sacred Walking Stick works?"

"Yes, my granddaughter. But there is more, much more to it than just that. But for now, I'll take the Stick and you can go out and join your friends."

"Why can't you tell me now what else the Sacred Walking Stick can do?" Sartaya asked.

"When I am ready to tell you more, I will. For now, it's important that you remember all you have learned today. Think about it and dream about it often. Your life will forever change as a result of what happened here today. Go now and find your friends."

CHAPTER 18

Sartaya, Yukawe, and Nakia spent the next day hanging out at the practice range. "I can't believe today is almost over," Sartaya said. "Grandfather wants to take both of you with him to search for other hunting grounds that are a little more than half of a day's travel from camp. It sounds like so much fun."

"How much longer is your grandmother going to train you? I know it's important. Wakishtay told me it is. But it's different being with your grandfather and Nakia without you. I miss having you with me . . . I mean us."

"Grandmother said my training will take as long as it takes. She said she would know when I've learned as much as I need to. I really miss being with the three of you, too."

The next morning during breakfast Sartaya asked her grandmother, "What kinds of plants will we be looking for today?" Sartaya noticed a slight mischievousness in her grandmother's eyes.

"Today, and everyday from now on, we will be doing things differently. I won't be telling you what kind of plant to find or where to find it. I will tell you what condition we want to treat. Then, it will be up to your spirit to show you the tree, bush, or plant and how to gather, prepare, and use it to treat this condition."

"But, Grandmother, I won't know what you're talking about. How will I find something that I don't know anything about? You have to show me so I can learn."

"Be still, Granddaughter. Have you already forgotten that you are now a medicine woman? Everything you need to know is already inside of you. You must learn how to pull the necessary information out when you need it. This is the only way. This is the way that I learned. This is the way that my mother and her mother before her learned. No more complaining."

"I'm sorry, Grandmother. This is all so new to me. I'm still confused about what happened the other day."

"I know, Sartaya. You're only eleven summers old. But there was a very good reason why the spirits of our ancestors decided it was time for you to be filled with their knowledge of medicine. They told me you are the youngest medicine woman of all time. When I was thirteen, I had the same questions you have now. It was then they told me there is no age requirement for being able to help other people. You must respect the Ancients, for they have wisdom and knowledge of the past, present, and future beyond our understanding. It is my responsibility to help you be ready for that time when your skills as a medicine woman will be needed; regardless of how old you may be at the time."

Miantra smiled. "Today and for many tomorrows, we will gather many different medicines that you can prepare and store for later use. These medicines will be yours, just as Maskanini and I have collected our own and have stored them for when we needed them to treat our people. I have spoken to your grandfather about our ancient ancestors visiting with you the other day. He was very happy for you. He will share this information with KiaNeeishtay today. I also told Wakishtay about your encounter with the Ancients, including Walking Stick. He, too, was happy for you. You have two grandfathers who couldn't be more proud of you. For now, no one else will be told about this. You are not to tell anyone about what happened to you. Otherwise, people may form unreasonable expectations of your medicinal and healing abilities. The time will come soon enough when people will seek you out to help them in any way that you can. For now, you must learn how to draw upon these skills using the knowledge that your ancestors have given to you."

Miantra rose and stepped out of her shelter. "To start, let's find some plants that will treat fevers. I'll give you a hint. Just as there are several different kinds of plants that will treat wounds and help people get some rest, there are several plants that can be used to treat fevers."

Having said that, the two medicine women strode out of camp together; one weathered and wrinkled hand holding onto another smaller and smoother hand.

CHAPTER 19

Much of that summer and fall, Sartaya, with the help of her grandmother, discovered the medicinal value of the wide variety of plants available in their region. Miantra was astonished by how quickly her granddaughter learned all of the different uses for many of these plants. *She listens well to her ancestral spirits.* By late fall, Sartaya had collected many of her own medicinal plants and was storing them in her grandparents' shelter.

Sartaya realized their personal shelter was fast becoming too crowded with the addition of her collection of medicinal plants to that of Maskanini and her grandmother. *It's already crowded in here with three people and a full-sized wolf.*

"Would it make sense, Grandmother, to build another shelter to store all of our medicines? There are many more plants and roots that my spirits have shown me that we can use to treat and heal our people, but I didn't want to bring them home because we don't have the room to store them. Another shelter would give us room to spread out and be more comfortable in here, especially when we have visitors. You and Grandfather never complained or said a word to me about Nakia taking up more room as he grew larger, for which I will always be grateful."

"I'll discuss your idea with Maskanini tonight."

Maskanini agreed that a special shelter to store and prepare all of their medicinal plants was a good idea. Several days later, after conferring with KiaNeeishtay and getting his permission, the three of them began building the additional shelter. Others, upon learning what they were planning, were more than willing to help gather the building materials for this special medicine shelter and also help with building it. Everyone, including KiaNeeishtay thought it was a great idea to have an abundance of medicinal plants on-hand. He also sympathized with how crowded Maskanini's shelter had become over the past several summers, especially with a full grown wolf living with them.

The new structure was built and finished in three days. It stood within twelve paces of their shelter. There were three distinct areas within the new structure to hold each of their individual medicinal plant collections. A fire ring was located in the center. An area to the side of the fire ring was set up for the preparation of various medicines. It contained several flat stone slabs, some broken clam shells, and specially formed stones used to strip, mash, and crush the different parts of plants.

There were also several clay-fired pots of different sizes for boiling water and mixing ingredients in. Several stick-racks used to dry plants were set up on another side of the fire ring. Underground storage holes were dug at the base of each of their individual areas. These holes were two arm lengths deep and covered by a thick woven mat of various grasses. Many of the medicinal roots were kept in these earthen storage holes until needed. The cooler holes kept many of these plants fresher and more usable for longer periods of time. Over time, some of these plants and their roots would have to be replaced with fresh ones.

CHAPTER 20

Sartaya's twelfth and thirteenth summer of life provided ample opportunities for the stored medicines to be used. She accompanied her grandparents whenever they were asked to help tribal members who were ill. She watched and learned much as Miantra and Maskanini treated the men, women, and children of the Natayeh for a wide variety of ailments. She admired how compassionate, understanding, and respectful her grandparents were of the people needing their care. She witnessed how this kindness seemed to calm and help the overall disposition and healing of those being treated. This invaluable experience helped strengthen her own attributes which were already becoming well-known within her tribe.

Half-way through Sartaya's twelfth winter, Maskanini and Miantra decided to give their granddaughter the opportunity to decide on possible treatments. In most cases, they didn't have to change her diagnosis or method of treatment. In others, she would recommend a method of treatment that neither of them had ever heard of or used before. After conferring with one another though, they usually agreed that their granddaughter's choice of treatment was as good, if not better, than what they would have chosen.

By the end of that twelfth winter, most people, through first-hand knowledge or word-of-mouth, knew of Sartaya's special medicinal skills. Her grandparents gave up trying to keep her newly acquired skills a secret only among close family members and the tribal leader. They were getting older and it was getting more difficult for them with each passing winter to care for the tribe's health needs. It made them feel good that their medicinal skills were now being passed on to this very capable soon-to-be young woman who just happened to be their granddaughter. They could not have been more proud of her.

One early morning of Sartaya's thirteenth summer of life, she stopped by Wakishtay's shelter to drop Nakia off. Wakishtay, Yukawe, and Nakia planned on spending most of the day hunting. Miantra planned to make clay pots and cups and had asked Sartaya to help her.

It was still fairly early in the morning when Miantra and her granddaughter arrived at the area set aside for making pottery. The fire pits had been emptied by the prior users.

"Sartaya, why don't you start a fire in the pit while I begin preparing the clay?" Sartaya nodded and started building the fire using some of the wood that had been stacked by prior users. After tending it a while, she said, "The fire is burning very hot, Grandmother."

"Good. Now help me with the clay." She poked a finger at a stiff, gray mass. "We're going to have to get some water to soften the clay." They each grabbed a water bag and headed for the stream.

I wonder what Grandfather, Yukawe, and Nakia are doing right now. I'll bet they're having more fun than I am Sartaya thought to herself.

I know she's day-dreaming about being with Wakishtay, but she'll enjoy herself once we get started. "That's it. Pour the water into the clay pit and I'll do the same." After piling the hard chunks of clay into the pit, Miantra watched as Sartaya worked the clay until it became soft and pliable.

"I think mine is as soft as I can get it. What do you think, Grandmother?" Miantra squeezed the clay with her aging hands and it squished through her fingers.

They both flattened out their chunks of clay. Then they reached into a pile of crushed clam shells stored nearby and sprinkled a handful of the dust over the top and bottom surface of their flattened clay. Then they worked more dust into the clay. It would help make the pottery harder and more resistant to breaking, once it was fired.

Now, they were ready to make something out of the clay. "Are you ready to make some cups and jars, Sartaya?" Miantra asked.

"I guess so," Sartaya replied, still not too enthused about any of this. They spent the rest of the day working the clay and fire heating what they created.

When they were finished, Miantra said, "Sartaya, we must come back here early tomorrow morning to clean up so that others will find it in the same condition as we did."

The next morning, both Sartaya and her grandmother returned to prepare the work area for whoever would use it next. "Sartaya, you clean out all the ashes from the pit while I gather more branches and high grass to replace what we've used."

"Okay, Grandmother, but when I'm finished with the pit, I'll help you." Miantra smiled at her granddaughter's thoughtfulness. It didn't take long before Sartaya had finished spreading the ashes from the pit to the surrounding area. "Grandmother, I'm finished cleaning the fire pit. Where are you?"

Sartaya thought it odd when her grandmother didn't answer. She searched the entire work area, looking for her. "Grandmother, where are you?" As she made her way around the large pile of brush used for the fire, she found Miantra lying on the ground. The girl smiled and said, "Are you hiding from me? I see you." But Miantra didn't move. In between her grandmother's listless body and a stack of wood was a large snake.

"Grandmother!"

Sartaya's mind filled with horrific images of this snake attacking her grandmother. *What should I do? What can I do? Was Grandmother bitten by the snake? How can I get this snake away from her? She's going to die if I don't do something!* The large snake didn't appear to be afraid of her. She yelled at it and moved toward it several times in a threatening manner, but it didn't move. "I have to get a large branch and try pushing it away," she thought out loud.

She picked up a thin branch half again as long as her body, then jabbed it at the snake. The snake moved a little, then returned to the same spot or even closer to her grandmother's body. This just didn't make any sense to Sartaya, who by now was terrified that her grandmother was dying. "Should I run to find Maskanini or Wakishtay? I don't know where they are right now. If I leave

Grandmother lying here, the snake will probably bite her again and again until she is dead!"

For a brief moment, Sartaya felt frustrated, "Why is this happening? I don't know what to do. I love my grandmother and don't want anything bad to happen to her," she cried as she slumped to the ground. Once again, her arm became inflamed where Nakia's mother had bitten her. The pain was intense as she automatically reached to rub it, hoping that would lessen the throbbing pain. After a moment or two, she cleared her mind of any unnecessary clutter and remembered what her ancient ancestors had told her only a short time ago. Out of desperation, she asked them for their help. Immediately, she became aware of Spirit Whispers instructing her on what she should be doing to save her grandmother's life. She had a hard time believing some of what they said.

She looked directly into the snake's eyes and realized that the snake was protecting the older woman from other predators. It knew who Sartaya was, but it couldn't clearly communicate its intentions to her. Her grandmother could communicate with animals, reptiles, and birds. She must have been talking with the snake before she collapsed and passed out. The snake had stayed around to protect her. "But what is wrong with Grandmother?" she asked herself.

Her ancient ancestors suggested what to check for. Without thinking, Sartaya placed her hand on Miantra's throat. She felt a weak pulse coursing through her grandmother's main blood vessel. "She's still alive," Sartaya concluded.

She then bent down and placed her ear next to the woman's mouth. She detected only a slight breath. The older woman wasn't getting enough air to regain consciousness. "How can I help her to take deeper breaths?" she wondered.

A vision came to her. Move away from my grandmother so I have more room, she said to the snake without speaking. The snake understood her unspoken words and moved away from the human it was protecting. Sartaya straddled the old woman's body and carefully sat on her chest. She then raised herself and her weight off of the woman. She did this six more times and then slapped the woman's cheeks with controlled force. Every time Sartaya put her weight on her grandmother's chest, she detected some air coming out of her mouth. She continued to perform this crude resuscitation maneuver many more times on the woman she loved so deeply. Finally, Miantra's breathing began to pick up and her breaths were deeper. She slowly opened her eyes and smiled at her granddaughter. She then turned her gaze toward the snake. "I see that you have met my friend," she said to Sartaya.

"Grandmother, what happened to you?"

"I was visiting with my friend, the snake, when all of a sudden I couldn't breathe right and fainted. I guess I'm getting old, Sartaya. But don't worry. I won't be leaving you soon. Help me to get up. Thank you, Sartaya. You saved my life. On the way back to our shelter you can tell me what you did to help me breathe better and wake up. Did I fall on my face? My cheeks really hurt."

Later that day Maskanini listened intently to the two of them describing what had happened. He had almost lost the most important person in his life. With a tearful smile, he wrapped his arms tightly around his granddaughter and whispered, "Sartaya, thank you for giving me back your grandmother. I will never forget what you have done." He then embraced his lifelong mate and held onto her tightly; not wanting to ever let her go. "I am so glad that you are here in my arms, again. I cannot bear the thought of losing you. I love you so deeply." Now, there were tears flowing down the cheeks of all three. "You really did slap your grandmother's cheeks," he said to Sartaya with a knowing smile as he noticed the puffy redness on his mate's face.

CHAPTER 21

For several full moons KiaNeeishtay had been promising his tribe he would be the storyteller at one of the evening campfires. A mild winter had passed, and the first signs of spring appeared as trees and plants began to bud. Because of the milder weather, more people began attending the evening campfires.

Finally, one late afternoon, the leader of the Natayeh announced that he would be the storyteller at the evening's campfire. Excitement filled the hearts of his people. By early evening, as the sun slowly receded into the western horizon, a roaring fire was in place. The majority of the tribe had already seated themselves around the fire while waiting in great anticipation for their leader to arrive.

KiaNeeishtay was pleased to see the smiles and excitement on everyone's faces as he walked up. He raised his hands to the evening sky. Only the crackling from the fire broke the ensuing silence surrounding the leader of the Natayeh. "We welcome the spirits of our ancestors to join us. We thank the Great Spirit for giving us a mild winter and the promise of an early spring." KiaNeeishtay now looked over all who had gathered with a satisfied look on his face, the Natayeh leader began his story.

"Many summers ago, about twenty-four members of the Natayeh were traveling a long distance to visit another tribe. A full moon into the trip, Wakishtay, had been tracking some deer and had come across the footprints of at least seven men. 'Someone has been watching us. This can't be good. I think I'll follow these tracks and see if I can spot them. Maybe I can learn what they're up to,' he thought to himself. He continued to follow the trail for awhile, then suddenly stopped when he heard men talking loudly. Very carefully and quietly he crawled towards them.

"The seven men were whooping and hollering and stumbling around their campfire. Their faces and bare arms were streaked with red paint. Their behavior was very erratic. As Wakishtay looked carefully over their small campsite, he spotted an extra spear leaning against one of the nearby trees. There was no mistaking the markings on this spear. It belonged to one of his own tribe. It was Trail Finder's spear, one of the two men sent ahead of the rest of the traveling Natayeh.

"Wakishtay understood something terrible had happened to Trail Finder. 'Why are they so close to our tribe? I'll stay here and watch them, and listen. Maybe I will learn something. They can hardly stand up!'

"When darkness finally surrounded all of them, Wakishtay stole away from their small camp. The seven men had been passed out for awhile. Wakishtay had overheard them bragging about how they had killed Trail Finder. Now, they were planning to steal two of the Natayeh women and kill several of the tribe's men. Chills ran up and down Wakishtay's spine. 'I must get back to my tribe and warn them of the danger,' he thought to himself. Other thoughts had entered his mind as well; thoughts of revenge for the murder of Trail Finder. 'I would like nothing better than to sneak up on every one of them while they are sleeping and kill them. But if I fail, then my tribe wouldn't know what they are planning or the fate of Trail Finder. No. I must return to my camp and warn them that they are in grave danger.'

"Once he arrived back at the Natayeh's temporary campsite, Wakishtay went directly to his tribal leader, KiaNatay, and explained what he had seen and heard. Even though most tribal members were already in their shelters for the night, KiaNatay sent out several men to summon them all to the main campfire. As soon as they had all gathered around the glowing embers, he and Wakishtay shared the disturbing news with the rest of the tribe. KiaNatay then set a plan into place that included hiding some of his strongest men at key places on the outskirts of their temporary camp early the next morning. The remaining men would keep themselves heavily armed while they busied themselves with routine tasks around the camp to make it appear as though no one in the camp suspected anything dire was about to happen.

"He then asked the women who were gathered around him for two volunteers to play an important role in his plan of deception. All the women raised their hands to help. However, two women stepped forward and insisted on playing the dangerous but necessary roles. One of the women was the leader's mate, Kyashee, and the other was Wakishtay's mate, Waawaatesi. The two men couldn't have been more proud of their mates.

"Grave concern for their safety filled his heart as he spoke to them. 'At least two of these strangers will march right into our camp, grab you, and force you to go with them. But we will never let them take you out of this camp. They may be rough on you, but I don't believe they will try to harm you while you are still in our camp. These men are not thinking clearly, though. Wakishtay has already told us that they are walking unsteadily and acting very erratic. They have covered their faces and arms with war paint. Their intentions are clear. They intend to harm us.

"The two of you, who have volunteered, must make sure you have your knives on you and hidden from their view. When you hear me whistle, you must act quickly. Pull out your knives and stab them deeply either in their legs or arms. They will not anticipate your attack. When they loosen their grip on you get away from them in any way that you can. We won't need much time for our spears to find their targets. Thank you again for doing this.' KiaNatay turned to the other women, 'Stay out of sight so that only these two women, Kyashee and Waawaatesi, can be easily observed and grabbed by the intruders.'

"KiaNatay then gathered the men who were to hide on the outskirts of their camp early that next morning. 'Do not let these murderers shoot their arrows into our camp. Kill each of them quickly and quietly so their brothers will not know what happened to them. Remember, they murdered Trail Finder. Show them no mercy.'

"No one from the Natayeh slept that night for fear the intruders might come earlier than expected. Before the morning's first hint of light, the designated Natayeh men were positioned and well hidden from view around the outer fringe of their campsite . . . waiting . . . ."

KiaNeeishtay paused to build anticipation. Then, he resumed his story. "As the Natayeh pretended to be breaking camp to continue their journey, two strangers, fully armed with bows slung over their shoulders, knives in their sheaths, hatchets hanging from their rawhide belts, and spears in hand swaggered into the campsite. Their faces and bare arms were streaked with red paint. They strutted right past the leader of the Natayeh, ignoring the tradition of asking permission to enter another tribe's campsite.

"Two of the Natayeh women appeared to be working together in the center of the camp folding the sides of one of the shelters. None of the other tribal women were visible. It had not been very long since the first rays of the morning sun. The two intruders, ignoring everyone else in the camp, headed straight toward these two women. When they reached their quarry, the two men viciously grabbed the women by their hair, then dragged the startled women toward the direction where they had first entered the camp site. One of the intruders yelled, 'Don't be foolish! We didn't come alone. We have warriors positioned all around you! If anything happens to either one of us, all of you will be slaughtered. We came only for these two worthless women. Now, get out of our way!'

"The one who yelled then turned around and faced the wooded area from which he first emerged. With a wicked smile, he raised his hand as if to signal something to the unseen others. 'Killing several of these wretched people will scare the others away from trailing us' his treacherous mind thought. A few moments passed. Nothing happened. 'What are they waiting for?' he thought. Both intruders were puzzled as to why no one in the camp had been shot yet. 'Shoot now!' The one intruder, frustrated, raised his hands and shouted again, 'Now! Shoot them now!' Suddenly, everyone heard a shrill whistle.

"The two outsiders glanced anxiously at one another. An unexpected feeling of dread coursed through their veins. Their thoughts merged and became one. 'What happened? Where are the others? Why aren't their arrows killing some of these worthless people?'

"In an instant, the two captive women slid their hands over the hidden, leather sheaths holding their knives. One of them stabbed her captor deep into his right thigh while the other turned and buried her knife deep into the flesh of the upper arm that held her hair. Both men shrieked in pain and surprise as they let go; a mistake that cost both of them their lives.

"Suddenly, they felt naked and vulnerable standing alone amongst the angry tribe whose camp they had just violated. That was to be the last emotion either one of them would feel. Four spears thrown with great strength and accuracy brought the two captors to their knees. Reflex caused their hands to tightly clasp the two protruding shafts of wood which held the sharpened flint spearheads buried deep in each of their chests. Their life force drained quickly. Their last heartbeat delivered only darkness to their eyes as their bodies slumped to the ground. The five remaining rogues had met an earlier but similar fate. Their eyes would never witness another sunrise."

The hearts of everyone gathered around the campfire raced as their leader concluded his story. This story had been told many times by KiaNeeishtay's father, KiaNatay, when he was the Natayeh tribal leader. Then after his untimely death, his son KiaNeeishtay, who was appointed leader of the Natayeh to replace his father, also repeated the story from time to time. Of course, Wakishtay was always asked to help fill in the details whenever questions were asked. Just twelve summers old, KiaNeeishtay had been with his mother and father on that fateful trip. His Father, KiaNatay, had wanted him to experience a trip of this magnitude, confident that his son was ready for the challenges such a long trip presented. After all, KiaNatay's father and mother had taken him on one of those trips soon after he had celebrated his eleventh summer of life.

KiaNeeishtay thought retelling this story now to all of his tribe's men, women, and children was timely. The very tribe that his father, mother, and he had visited in the story were now on their way to visit with the Natayeh. Two men from the Zakenaque—*Smokey Mountain*

Tribe—had just arrived earlier that day to give the Natayeh advance notice of their tribe's arrival within one full moon. These visits between both tribes had been occurring for more generations than either tribe's elders could remember. KiaNeeishtay also wanted to impress upon his people how difficult and dangerous these trips could sometimes be. He felt that any tribe that decides to make such a trip was courageous and should be treated with great respect.

Sartaya beamed with pride every time this story was told. After all, it was her Grandfather Wakishtay and her Grandmother Waawaatesi who showed tremendous courage throughout the story. She had never met her Grandmother Waawaatesi, who had died unexpectedly before she was born. *I hope when I grow up, I will have the same kind of courage Waawaatesi had when she was assaulted by those intruders. She was so brave to volunteer. I wonder if she was scared at all.*

CHAPTER 22

Much excitement had filled the air since the announcement that the Zakenaque were on their way to visit with the Natayeh. The visitors' homeland was named after the dense fogs and low clouds that often surrounded the high hills and mountains of that region. The magnificent valleys in the area were home to a wide variety of many of the same kinds of animals that thrived in the area surrounding the Natayeh. However, the minerals and rocks were quite different from those found close to the Natayeh. Because of its hardness, the flint from this region was considered superior for arrow and spear points.

About a third of the Zakenaque had begun their long journey in the early spring. They hoped to arrive sometime in the middle of the summer. The twenty-seven visitors, mostly male and female adults along with a few older children, planned to visit with the Natayeh for several full moons before returning in the early fall.

In early summer, KiaNeeishtay began sending out several scouts every six to eight days looking for signs that the Zakenaque visitors were coming. The scouts usually included at least one of the two Zakenaque who had arrived earlier. KiaNeeishtay knew that when tribes traveled such long distances they could arrive quite a bit earlier or later than had been originally planned. In any case, he wanted to be prepared for his guests when they finally arrived. He had a beautiful spot just outside their encampment cleared for the visitors to use for their shelters and fires. He also provided several large piles of aging wood for his guests. Within a stone's throw of this cleared area was a slow-moving stream that would provide their visitors with plenty of drinking, cooking, and bathing water.

KiaNeeishtay also planned a large banquet to celebrate the Zakenaque's arrival. He knew that the travelers, after eating small meals while making their long journey would appreciate the banquet. The entire tribe joined together to prepare for this visit and to make it a memorable one for all. They even enlarged their main campfire site to make room for additional guests. Fortunately, there was an abundance of game, fish, and plant food in the area, enough for each tribe's needs.

Lakato, known throughout the region for his quality spears, had been busy for more than a full moon making arrows and spears for trading. They would all have his trademark artwork carved into them. Wakishtay, along with other tribal hunters, had been asked to prepare many animal hides for trading. Maskanini and KiaNeeishtay were busy preparing for a special ceremony to honor their guests.

Many of the women made necklaces and bracelets out of animal and bird bones, as well as local stones and shells to be given as gifts or traded. Others had been very busy making fired clay cups, bowls, and pots for their guests to use. The visitors would not have brought any of their own pottery. Both its weight and brittleness would make it too difficult to carry on a long journey.

Large areas outside of the main encampment were being prepared for games and contests. In some cases, the Natayeh women would have a distinct advantage over most females of any visiting tribe because some of them, by choice, learned how to hunt. In most other tribes, men usually did all the hunting, while the women took care of gathering plant foods. The Natayeh would have to be careful not to offend or embarrass their guests, but at the same time show them the advantages of the Natayeh's ways. In any event, men would compete against men, women against women, and children against children. KiaNeeishtay smiled as he pondered the possibilities and different scenarios that would most likely occur.

While the tribe was busily preparing for their visitors, Sartaya, Nakia, and Yukawe were inseparable. It didn't seem to any of them that much time had passed since their ordeal with the mountain lion. Sartaya had already added the thirteenth and final turquoise stone to her Necklace of Age. The following summer she would be considered a young woman and would choose an appropriate Life Necklace to replace her Necklace of Age. Yukawe was fifteen summers old and was now considered a young man. The two of them usually spent most of their time at the training site practicing with their bows and arrows, as well as with their spears. Sartaya also shared with Yukawe much of what her grandmother had been teaching her about gathering various plants and their roots for both food and medicinal purposes. She had not told him about her Spirit Dreams and visitations by her ancient ancestors who declared her to be a medicine woman. Yukawe considered her his best friend. Recently, however, his feelings towards her were changing. He wanted to be more than just her friend as he noticed her becoming a young woman. *She is beautiful*, he thought to himself with an admiring smile.

CHAPTER 23

One day after several men went out to look for signs of the visitors, they came back to camp accompanied by two additional scouts from the Zakenaque. The scouts excitedly announced that their tribe would arrive in about fourteen days. That evening, KiaNeeishtay announced at the tribal camp fire, "Our guests will be here ahead of schedule and are only fourteen days away. In eleven days, the designated hunters will leave to hunt and bring back as many deer and other animals as they can carry back to camp." The leader of the Natayeh then turned to Maskanini and nodded. Maskanini rose and looked upward.

He raised his hands toward the many sparkling stars that filled the evening sky. "We call upon our ancestors to help guide our hunters and help them find plentiful game. We will soon have many extra mouths to feed and do not want to disappoint our guests. Help our arrows and spears to fly true so that the spirits of these animals will not suffer. We are thankful for their sacrifice." As Maskanini sat down, everyone chattered excitedly to one another about their own plans to prepare for this special visit. It was late in the evening by the time the last of the stragglers finally left the glowing embers of the campfire for their shelters. After a restful night and a filling morning meal, two of the scouts and two volunteers from the Natayeh left camp to rejoin the traveling Zakenaque and let them know that all was well with the hosting tribe and that they would be welcomed. The other two visitors stayed behind to help the Natayeh to prepare for their tribe's arrival.

The excitement within the tribe grew as each new day brought them closer to when their visitors would arrive. No one felt as though something was missing or wasn't going to get done in time for their visitors. By the thirteenth day, all preparations for their guests were completed. The next day, the visitors would arrive.

Halfway through the next day's afternoon, the two Natayeh volunteers that had joined the two Zakenaque scouts came running into camp shouting excitedly, "They're coming! They'll be here shortly!" Both old and young stopped whatever it was that they were doing and went to gather just outside their camp grounds. There, they waited to welcome the Zakenaque members who had traveled several full moons over a great distance in order to visit with them.

Sartaya, Nakia, Wakishtay, Maskanini, and Miantra stood together. KiaNeeishtay and his mate, Miikwasi, stood next to them. Yukawe, Lakato, and Bosaata also stood close by. Much excitement filled the air as members of the visiting tribe began to come into view. There was much howling and shrieking and hand waving by the excited host tribal members.

As the Zakenaque members came to within a few hundred paces of the camp, the Natayeh leader and his mate walked out to greet the leader of the Zakenaque. "Welcome. I am KiaNeeishtay, leader of the Natayeh. This is my mate, Miikwasi."

"Thank you for inviting us to visit. I am Keenatay, leader of the Zakenaque."

"You've traveled far to visit the Natayeh. Let us help you in setting up your shelters. Once you've settled in, you and your people are invited to join us in a 'welcoming feast'. Afterwards, just before the sun disappears, there will be a ceremony at our main campfire to honor you and your people. Let me help you carry some of your belongings to the area my people have prepared for you and your tribe."

"I'm grateful for your help. It's been a long and tiring journey. Please, lead the way."

After the leaders greeted one another, the rest of the Natayeh hurried to meet their visitors. As the host tribe intermingled with their guests they offered to help carry some of their belongings to the newly prepared campsite. As Maskanini and Miantra headed toward their guests, three others remained behind. Wakishtay, Sartaya, and Nakia didn't move. They had previously discussed this moment with both Maskanini and Miantra, as well as with KiaNeeishtay. All agreed it would be best if they let their visitors slowly get used to the fact that one of the Natayeh tribal members was a wolf. Nevertheless, Sartaya found it hard to stay behind.

Many members of the visiting tribe gasped when they glanced toward the old man, the girl, and the wolf. Some of them thought they recognized the old man as someone who had once visited them many summers ago. Most of them were relieved they didn't have to go any closer to the wolf. Sartaya hugged her brother and whispered, "You'll have to be on your best behavior until they get used to you. But don't worry, that won't take long." Sartaya planned to visit the guest tribe with many of the Natayeh children and Nakia. *Once they see how the Natayeh children have taken to my Nakia, they will quickly get over their fear and accept Nakia as their friend.*

The visitors were guided around the perimeter of the main camp to the newly prepared grounds that would serve as the Zakenaque's campsite. The visitors were elated with the site, a slightly elevated stretch of level ground overlooking a wide, slow-moving stream. They all thought it was perfect.

The Natayeh helped their guests erect their shelters and then excused themselves. There was much to be done back at their own camp to prepare for the feast and welcoming ceremony that evening. The Zakenaque members were grateful for their help. As their hosts left, they each began to organize the rest of their belongings into and around their shelters making themselves as comfortable as possible. Many took the opportunity to rest for a short time. *We're finally here. That was one long trip. Was that a wolf standing by the young girl and the old man? There's something familiar about the old man,* one of the older men thought just before he nodded off.

CHAPTER 24

It was early evening when the Natayeh leader sent Maskanini, Miantra, and Miikwasi over to the Zakenaque's campsite to invite them to the welcoming feast. They walked directly up to their guests' leader, Keenatay, who had just finished helping others stack firewood for their individual campfires. "Do your people have everything they need? Are you comfortable with the grounds?" asked Maskanini.

"Yes. Thank you for everything."

"The feast celebrating your arrival is ready. Come, follow us."

KiaNeeishtay and the rest of his tribe stood in parallel lines facing one another. The Natayeh leader motioned for his guests to enter between the two lines. As they did they were directed to where the food sat on crude makeshift tables. The guests were to have first choice. There was certainly plenty to go around. The Natayeh hunters had been very successful. There was deer, rabbit, squirrel, turkey, and several varieties of fish. There were also many edible leafy plants, mushrooms, and roots. No one will go hungry this night, thought KiaNeeishtay.

Once their guests had taken what they wanted and sat down wherever it was convenient to eat, the Natayeh leader gave his people a nod to help themselves to the banquet. After he had gotten his food, KiaNeeishtay went over to where Keenatay was sitting. "I will join you if that is alright?"

"Yes." Those close to their leader moved over to make more room for KiaNeeishtay. "The food is plentiful and very good. Thank you," Keenatay exclaimed.

"Please help yourselves. There is more than enough for everyone to have as much as they want." With that said, Keenatay smiled and stood up to help himself to more food. Seeing their leader go back was all the encouragement some of his tribal members needed to also help themselves to seconds. This made KiaNeeishtay very happy. Everything is going well, he thought. I can only hope the rest of their visit goes as well.

The leader of the Zakenaque soon returned with his second helping. The Natayeh leader smiled. "After the meal, when the first signs of darkness appear, please join us at our campfire. We would like to celebrate your safe arrival and honor your people for their bravery and courage in making such a long journey. I promise it won't take long. I know your people must be very tired and ready for a good night's rest. They can stay around the campfire as long as they want. We won't be offended if they want to get back to their shelters to collapse." The two leaders laughed.

"There will be much food left from tonight's feast. I invite your people to take as much food back to their shelter to store as they need for meals during the next several days. Tomorrow, in the afternoon, we'll organize hunting groups of our hunters and yours. In two days, we'll show you our favorite hunting grounds. There should be plenty of animals to feed both of our tribes. Oh, and there are many lakes and streams to hunt fish, as well. Our women will get together with yours and show them where they can gather mushrooms, roots, and greens."

"You have thought of everything and are a very good host," Keenatay said to the Natayeh leader. The two men smiled at each other respectfully.

"I'm going to get another helping of food and make sure my people have everything they need," KiaNeeishtay said. "I will see you tonight at the campfire." Keenatay nodded in agreement.

It was a perfect evening for a ceremonial campfire to honor their Zakenaque guests. KiaNeeishtay invited Keenatay to join him and he respectfully agreed. Maskanini, Miantra, Sartaya, Nakia, and Wakishtay sat next to the Natayeh leader on his left side. Many of the guests murmured to one another when they spotted the wolf resting so close to KiaNeeishtay. Keenatay had to walk past the five of them and as he did, KiaNeeishtay introduced him to each of them, including the wolf. "This is Nakia, brother to Sartaya. I will explain how this came to be later tonight. This is my mother, Kyashee, sitting to my right. Please, sit between us."

Keenatay nodded out of respect for his host but wasn't quite sure what to make of the wolf, although it did seem well behaved. He was somewhat relieved when KiaNeeishtay asked him to sit next to him on his right between him and his mother. Sitting to the right of a tribal leader was considered an honor and usually had to be earned over time. *I wonder why he asked me to sit to his right. Maybe, he just wanted me to feel more comfortable away from the wolf.*

Once everyone gathered around the campfire, KiaNeeishtay stood up and raised his hands. The only noise heard was the crackling from the fire. "Welcome, friends of the Zakenaque. The Natayeh have been looking forward to your visit for many moons. I was only twelve summers old when members of my tribe last visited you in your highland camp. My father, KiaNatay, who was our tribal leader then, thought it was time for me to make that great journey to your land. He was right. I will never forget how beautiful that part of the country was to me.

"My father has joined the Great Spirit and is smiling down on us right now. My mother, Kyashee who was also with us when we visited your village is sitting next to Keenatay.

"It took great courage for each of you to leave your homeland and make this journey to visit with us. It's a long time to be away from family and friends and the land that you call home. The Natayeh people recognize you for your courage." The Natayeh rose from where they had been sitting and cheered loudly for their guests. KiaNeeishtay raised his hands and his people sat back down. "We are honored to have all of you for our guests and as our friends." The sun-weathered cheeks of the visitors turned crimson as they were filled with pride at the words of the Natayeh tribal leader.

KiaNeeishtay nodded at Maskanini and sat down. Maskanini rose and asked both leaders to stand next to him. Miantra also stood, holding two bowls of colored paste. One contained a white paste, the other a blue. Looking to the evening sky, Maskanini asked the ancestors of both tribes to witness and approve the ceremony about to take place. "Grasp each other's right forearm with your right hand," he directed both leaders. "Great Spirit, these two leaders are each very strong and courageous. They declare their friendship to one another and are now even stronger and more courageous than they were as one." While saying this, he dipped one finger into the white paste and drew a single circle around the men's forearms. Then, dipping a second finger into the blue paste, he drew a second circle around their forearms. "It is done. Just as each leader is now stronger and more courageous, so too are the people of each tribe who they lead." Both tribes stood up and cheered loudly. Maskanini sat down.

KiaNeeishtay stood and raised his hands. There was silence once again around the campfire. "Some of you have probably noticed the wolf resting to my left. This is Nakia, Wolf Brother to Sartaya. Sartaya, please stand next to me with Nakia." She rose and stood next to her tribal leader. With a slight movement of her eyes, unnoticed by everyone else except for Wakishtay, Nakia rose and stood by his sister's side. "From the beginning of time, our tribe has always been named Natayeh, the Gray Wolf Tribe. Throughout the generations, we have always had the greatest respect for these animals. We have watched them from afar and have learned their ways. They are great hunters and providers for their packs.

"When Sartaya was only eight summers old, she wandered away from some of the women who had been gathering mushrooms. This was common for her. She always seemed to find some small baby animal to bring back to show the rest of us. Usually it was a rabbit, sometimes a turtle, and once in a while, a small snake." Everyone laughed, enjoying the story of this curious and mischievous little girl. "One morning she returned with a wolf pup. Of course, this concerned us because she could have been attacked by its parents. The wolf pup was brought back to our camp while Wakishtay returned to the site where Sartaya had found the pup. He discovered that its mother had died from a broken rib that had punctured her lungs.

"We asked the Great Spirit why He had brought this wolf pup into our lives. He then guided us to have a sacred ceremony declaring the wolf pup and Sartaya to be brother and sister. To this day, Nakia lives with Sartaya and her grandparents, Miantra and Maskanini. Wakishtay, who is also Sartaya's grandfather, is very close to the wolf, as well. The wolf considers him its pack leader. The Great Spirit thought it would be good for our tribe to have a wolf in it since we had named ourselves the Natayeh. Nakia has earned the love and respect of all members of the Natayeh. He will not harm any of you, but he will come to your aid if you are in danger. The children enjoy playing with him and he enjoys playing with them. So, please do not be afraid of him and treat him with the same respect as you have for the rest of us."

KiaNeeishtay then nodded to Miantra. She stood and smiled at everyone. "We have welcoming gifts for all of you. The women of the Natayeh have made bowls, pots, and cups for each of your shelters. They will deliver them to you tonight after you have returned to your campsite."

KiaNeeishtay stood and motioned to everyone that the official campfire and ceremony was over. KiaNeeishtay and Keenatay clasped each other's forearms completing the two colored circles painted on each of their arms. Then they both made their way to their individual shelters for the night.

CHAPTER 25

After several days, the visitor's camp ran low on vegetables. A small group of their women decided to return to the general area the Natayeh women had shown them when they had first arrived. This area abounded with edible mushrooms, roots, and leafy plants. As they didn't want to bother their hosts, six of them headed out early in the morning to gather whatever plant food they could find.

Their path went past the training area for bow hunting and spear throwing Wakishtay had originally prepared for Sartaya, but was now used by most of the tribe. Nakia heard the women approach long before they came near where Sartaya was repairing the grass targets. When they came upon the girl and her wolf, she politely asked them, "Do you mind if Nakia and I join you? I can show you where some of the best plants are located and help you gather them."

The women smiled at her, but seemed hesitant. Sartaya sensed they weren't comfortable with a wolf in their midst. One especially nervous woman asked if she could leave the wolf behind. Sartaya assured them Nakia wasn't a threat, but if they weren't comfortable with him being by her side, she and the Wolf would remain behind. The visitors nodded and continued on their way.

"Did you see the bow and arrows and spear that young girl carried?" one woman asked the others. They all nodded and murmured their misgivings.

A short distance away from the armed girl and her wolf one of the women spotted a berry patch just off the well-traveled path. She told the others she would gather berries while the rest of them foraged for roots and vegetables. They all smiled with delight at the thought of having fresh berries with their meals.

"We'll stop back for you in a little while," the rest shouted.

The woman who had spotted the berries was small and beautiful. She was strong-willed, yet respectful of others, and very skilled at making beautiful clothes. She was called Sabenta because she would get up before anyone else every morning to welcome the sun into her life. Everyone adored her, especially the man who led the Zakenaque. A skilled hunter, Keenatay had killed more Elk than any four hunters in his tribe put together. There was always great anticipation whenever he went hunting that he would bring back an elk. It was also anticipated that he and Sabenta would soon be together as mates.

While the rest foraged for vegetables, Sabenta picked blueberries, gathering them in an old hide. While thinking of all the wonderful ways to use the berries, a slight rustling sound told her she was not alone. She looked up. Off to her left and slightly ahead of her was the largest black bear she had ever seen. It too was foraging for berries.

Frightened, Sabenta slowly backed away. The bear smelled her fear. Already angry that she was in his territory, he lowered his head and moved it back and forth in a threatening manner while easing forward in her direction. He never took his eyes off her.

She tried to back up faster, but that only emboldened the huge bear to attack. As the frightened young woman turned to run, the bear's strong jaws clamped onto her left shoulder. He picked her up and flung her backwards in the air about fifteen paces. She screamed in pain, then landed hard on her left side. She tried to push herself up with her left hand, but couldn't. Her left arm hung limp, the tendons and muscle torn and exposed by the bear's attack.

Sabenta turned just in time to feel the bears claws slash deeply into her side. She screamed again, then passed out from the pain. The bear, thinking it now had its meal for the day, began to drag her limp body to a different place.

The young woman's screams did not go unnoticed, though. When Nakia heard the angry, low growling of a threatening animal, he sped ahead of Sartaya towards the sounds of the screams, not waiting for his sister's permission to leave. Sartaya followed him, running as fast as she could. She skidded to a stop when she heard the bear growling.

From behind a patch of high ground cover, she saw Nakia had charged in front of the bear to try and cut off its escape. The wolf bared his fangs and growled. The bear dropped Sabenta, then reared up on its hind legs to face this new threat. Nakia lunged forward, his jaws aimed for the bear's throat. The huge bear's claws raked deep gashes across the wolf's ribcage as it pried the wolf off its neck. Nakia howled in pain. Then, effortlessly, as if swatting a bug, the bear tossed him backwards into the air. Nakia crashed into a tree trunk, breaking several ribs, before slumping to the ground.

The bear looked over the unmoving wolf and decided it no longer posed a threat. It turned back to its earlier prey. Just as it was about to snatch up Sabenta the bear jerked upward and roared in pain and anger. An arrow protruded from the front of the bear's neck. The surprised creature spun around, trying to get a glimpse of this new threat, but saw nothing. Before it could identify the source of the danger, a second arrow pierced the front of his neck. This time, his blood squirted out in large quantities.

The wounded and confused animal turned around and stumbled. Fear replaced anger. The bear sensed survival depended on how fast he could retreat, but his legs wouldn't obey his commands to turn and run as fast as he could. It staggered away from the still bodies of the wolf and the young woman; its life force quickly ebbing from the fountain of blood gushing from its throat.

Once the bear was out of sight, Sartaya ran to her brother's side, crying for him to acknowledge her. The wolf bled from the deep gashes in its sides. Nakia was unconscious and barely breathing. Sartaya turned her attention to the woman attacked by the bear. She, too, was unconscious and bleeding from her wounds. She still breathed, although ever so faintly. Sartaya held her in her arms thinking she should go and get help. But, she didn't want to leave either of them in case the bear came back.

Just then the other women, who had heard the terrible screams, ran back to the berry patch. Horrified by the grotesque and bloody figure of their friend lying in Sartaya's arms, they first thought the wolf had attacked their friend. But then they noticed the injured wolf lying at the foot of a large tree trunk.

"What happened here?" one of the older women cried.

Sartaya, still a little dazed, said "Bear! Bear! A large black bear attacked your friend and my wolf."

"Where is the bear now?" Sartaya pointed in the direction the bear had gone.

"What if it comes back?" another woman cried hysterically. "We should leave this place now or we'll get attacked too!"

The oldest woman of the group told the others to run back to camp as quickly as they could and not to turn around, but to just keep running. "Get help! Now go, quickly!" The other women nodded and began to run as fast as they could back toward camp.

In the meantime, the woman who had stayed turned to Sartaya who was bloody from holding the injured young woman and the wounded wolf. "Tell me where you're hurt."

"I'm not hurt, but I'm afraid the bear has killed my brother."

"Your brother? But it's a wolf!"

"He's hurt so badly and in so much pain. What if the bear comes back? We won't be able to stop him from hurting us or taking your friend. Is she going to die?"

"I don't know," the older woman said. "She's hurt really bad." Sartaya left the injured woman and made her way over to Nakia's side. Meanwhile, the woman carefully lifted the injured woman's head and shoulders so they were resting in her lap. She hummed a tune while gently stroking Sabenta's bloodied and matted hair.

When the other women made it back, they began screaming to alert the others to the danger. Men from both tribes dropped what they were doing and rushed over. Once the women explained what happened, the men grabbed their weapons and raced towards the training area.

The older woman who had stayed behind had put pressure on some of Sabenta's wounds to slow the bleeding. Once the men arrived at the scene, one of them gently picked the injured woman up and headed back toward the encampment as fast as he could. The older woman rose and followed, trying to keep up as best she could.

Wakishtay, Lakato, and KiaNeeishtay quickly assessed the situation. Wakishtay immediately went over to Sartaya and knelt down beside her and Nakia. The Wolf looked badly hurt, maybe even dead. He embraced his granddaughter. She trembled while tears flooded her eyes and rolled down her tanned cheeks. "Oh, Grandfather. I think Nakia is dying."

In the meantime, Lakato and KiaNeeishtay, along with several members of the other tribe, started examining the path where the young woman had been attacked. They surmised what had happened, fearful the bear was still in the area and could return. There was blood everywhere.

KiaNeeishtay gathered up Nakia's limp body while Lakato lifted Sartaya. KiaNeeishtay motioned for the others to join them in returning to camp. As they did, all the men noted the area so they could return with a hunting party to kill the rogue bear. For once a bear attacks a human, it will not hesitate to attack them again.

While the men from the Zakenaque headed back toward their camp, KiaNeeishtay and Lakato left Sartaya and her injured wolf brother with Wakishtay and Miantra. Then, the two men organized a perimeter of hunters around their encampment in case the bear had followed them.

Miantra immediately recognized the seriousness of Nakia's injuries. Her mate, Maskanini, had already been told of Sabenta's injuries by Wakishtay and was on his way to the guest tribe's encampment to help her in any way that he could.

"Sartaya. Where are you hurt? You have blood all over you." Miantra anxiously examined her granddaughter from head to toe, looking for injuries that could have caused so much blood.

Wakishtay softly said, "She's not injured. The blood is from Nakia and the young woman attacked by the bear." Miantra breathed a deep sigh of relief, then turned her attention to Nakia.

"Sartaya, go to the stream and wash yourself and your clothes while your grandfather brings back some water. Go, quickly, both of you." Sartaya, still numb from everything that had happened was reluctant to leave her brother. "Please go with your grandfather, now," the girl's grandmother insisted. Reluctantly, Sartaya left with her grandfather and headed for the stream.

The water will help Sartaya clear her head for what she will have to do to help Nakia, Miantra thought. *And she'll need to bring back more fresh water to clean Nakia's wounds. After I'm done here, I need to help Maskanini treat that young woman.*

She tried to clear her mind so she could focus on saving the wolf's life. He was near dead. She felt along his ribcage and was shocked to feel so many broken ribs. Blood still oozed from the open wounds on his side. *Ah. But it's oozing slowly, which means his blood is thickening, unless he has bled out already!* She shuddered. *I wish Sartaya and her grandfather would hurry back soon. Oh, Nakia, please fight to live,* she pleaded. *Sartaya will do everything she can to help you on your journey back to us.*

She gently laid the wolf on its side and went to the medicinal shelter where they stored their medicine. Eventually, she found medicine she thought would help sterilize the wolf's wounds. *Sartaya will need fresh water to mix these ingredients into a paste to apply on the open wounds. The medicine will hurt when it comes into contact with his raw flesh, but the pain is part of the healing process. If he has no pain, well . . . then, it will be too late to help stave off the infection, and Nakia will join our ancestors in the sky.*

I'm glad he's unconscious. With the pain from all of his wounds, he probably would not be able to stand more pain brought on by the medicine. Just then, Sartaya and her grandfather returned from the stream. "How do you feel now?" she asked her granddaughter.

"I'm worried Nakia might die. Can you save him, Grandmother?"

Miantra held her tightly in her arms, whispering, "We'll do all we can to save him, but he is so badly injured. Perhaps you could ask the Great Spirit to help him."

Wakishtay looked desperate. "How can I help?"

"Nakia has many broken ribs," Miantra said. "If he lives, each broken bone will have to be reset, then held in place by tightly wrapping a hide around him. Sartaya, I must go help Maskanini care for the injured woman. You will have to mix these ingredients. Then, you'll need your grandfather's help in holding and turning Nakia so you can apply the mixture to the open wounds."

Sartaya looked at her grandmother in disbelief. "You're not going to leave us, are you?"

"Sartaya, you can do this," Miantra said looking directly into her granddaughter's eyes. "You are now a medicine woman. Look to your spirit for help. This is why your ancient ancestors chose you at such a young age to be a medicine woman. Remember, you have all the knowledge you will need to help Nakia. But if the Great Spirit wants Nakia by His side, then there is nothing that any of us can do." Miantra turned and left the shelter. After gathering most of Maskanini's medicines into a hide bag, she hurried toward Sabenta's shelter.

Wakishtay embraced his granddaughter. "We'll do everything we can to save Nakia. Maybe, it's time for you to call upon the spirit of Nakia's mother and ask for her help. We have both dreamed of things yet to come, and Nakia was with us in those dreams. I don't think he is supposed to leave us yet. And don't forget to ask your mountain lion's spirit to fill Nakia with his strength."

"Thank you, Grandfather, for reminding me of those spirits. I will ask them right now."

As she did, her arm flushed crimson red and caused her intense pain. But the pain helped clear her mind and focus more intently on what she needed to do to help her brother. Sartaya mixed the medicine in a bowl until the ingredients had a pasty consistency. Wakishtay noted the air of confidence and the determined look. The old man smiled. Her ancient spirits were now with her and guiding her every decision and action.

Then, he noticed the redness in her arm. "Sartaya, has the wound on your arm become infected again? Does it hurt?" he asked, alarmed.

"No. It only turns red and hurts when I have to do something important. I think it's caused by the spirit of Nakia's mother. Even though it's painful, it helps me concentrate and do my best at whatever I'm doing. Then it disappears, again."

Puzzled, the old hunter asked, "Did it get red and hurt when you made your first kill?"

"Yes. It did the same thing when I saved Nakia from the snare trap. And when I helped Grandmother breathe, it turned a painful red. The pain clears my mind of everything else except for what has to be done. It sharpens all my senses and takes away my fear."

Wakishtay nodded to to himself and wondered, "What does Great Spirit have in store for her? What will be her destiny, if not for something very important? Not only is she in touch with and being guided by the Ancients, but the Great Spirit has also asked the spirit of Nakia's mother to watch over her. The mountain lion's spirit is there for her, too. This is good, for I am too old to be of much help to her anymore."

Once the paste was ready, she turned to Wakishtay. "Please turn him on his side." As he did, Nakia shivered.

"Can you help me open the wounds as wide as possible?" Sartaya asked. Wakishtay obliged and she spread the mixture over the wounds. Then, they took turns pushing on the surrounding flesh, trying to drive the thick solution deeper into the injuries. They repeated the process until all the gashes were filled with the healing paste; some of it slowly oozing back out. Sartaya knew these wounds had to heal from the inside out. There would be no sewing needed to close the wounds. If anything, they would have to be filled continually with the healing paste over the next thirty days.

They rested Nakia on his back while Wakishtay returned to his shelter to look for a hide to wrap the injured wolf's ribcage once they had reset his broken bones. It didn't take him long to come back with a hide that could be cut into strips and tied around the wolf's body with handmade twine. The hard part was yet to come. Wakishtay knew Nakia's broken ribs would heal eventually, if he lived. But they had to be carefully reset, then held in place to fuse together successfully.

Wakishtay and Sartaya worked in unison to turn the wolf on his left side. This time, they both felt a slight shiver from the wolf's body. The old hunter ran his fingers along each rib. As he felt each broken bone, he maneuvered the bones back into place. His fingers throbbed with pain, but his love for Nakia overcame all of his discomforts. Each time he reset a rib, they both felt Nakia shudder. It hurt both of them to know that Nakia, even though unconscious, felt every painful adjustment. Tears escaped their hiding place and flowed down both their cheeks. They carefully positioned thin, flat pieces of bark from a river birch tree to each of the reset broken ribs. Then they tied some of the cut strips of hide around his body to secure the bark and keep it from moving.

Then it was time to turn Nakia over, to set the broken ribs on his other side. The two who had helped raise him from a pup were as gentle as they possibly could be. Even so, the shuddering from deep within the wolf told them he still felt the pain.

"Maybe it's good he's feeling pain," Sartaya said. "If he wasn't feeling anything, then he probably wouldn't have any chance at all." The old hunter nodded at her wisdom. When Sartaya completed resetting the remaining broken ribs, Wakishtay carefully tied more thin pieces of bark around them. Then, at Sartaya's suggestion, they gently laid Nakia on his mother's hide that he and Sartaya shared as bedding.

It was Keenatay who carried Sabenta back to camp. Seeing her wounds, his heart filled with despair. *She will soon be joining our ancestors.* As they approached her shelter, he yelled for someone to get Maskanini from the Natayeh. Several men bolted for the other encampment, running into Maskanini who was already heading for their camp. He rushed into her shelter without announcing himself. Upon seeing the young woman, Maskanini immediately felt for a pulse, fearing the worst. But he felt a very slight pulse. *How could she still be alive after suffering wounds like these?*

"Bring me fresh water from the stream," he commanded. If she had any chance of surviving, he would need all the knowledge he had acquired throughout his long life. He silently prayed, asking the Great Spirit for help.

Feeling helpless, but wanting to do something, Keenatay asked, "What can I do?"

"Please run back to my shelter and ask Miantra to bring all of my medicine as quickly as possible. I don't know if I can save Sabenta. Her wounds are so severe. But I promise you I'll do everything I can, and will stay by her side until we know one way or the other." Keenatay felt reassured by Maskanini's words.

He ran toward Maskanini's shelter to get Miantra. Halfway there, he spotted Miantra carrying a bulging hide. He stopped and asked if he could carry the hide for her and she nodded gratefully.

"How did you know I was coming for you?" he asked.

"I heard of the terrible attack on Sabenta from Wakishtay when he brought the injured wolf to my shelter. I knew Maskanini would need all of his medicine. Go. Run as fast as you can. These old legs will only slow you down. Tell Maskanini I'm on my way." He nodded, then took off running with the hide of medicines.

Maskanini was cleaning Sabenta's open wounds when Keenatay returned. "Is my mate coming?" he asked the young man.

"Yes. She was already on her way to you."

"Good. Clean some bowls. I'll need them for mixing up the medicines." The young man hurried down to the stream, then returned quickly with the clean bowls. Miantra had arrived in the meantime and was helping to wash the young woman's deep injuries.

Neither Maskanini nor his mate had ever seen such extensive injuries to a person's shoulder and body. It would take more than their combined skills to save her. Her life was in the Great Spirit's hands now. If He wanted her to live, then He would have to guide their hands to do what they had never done before. They both prayed silently and asked their ancient ancestral healers to help them.

Suddenly, the space within Keenatay's shelter filled with the spirits of ancient medicine men and women. Voices, speaking in many tongues, heard only by the two healers, offered helpful instructions and encouragement. As the sun began its descent, Maskanini and Miantra continued to put this woman's broken body back together. They scarcely talked to one another throughout the entire ordeal. Although, they seemed to be in a trance-like state, Keenatay simply assumed they each knew what the other wanted before being asked and just did it. He marveled at how they complimented one another. It was as if the Great Spirit guided their every action.

After cleaning and disinfecting Sabenta's injuries, they focused on the task of repairing her shoulder and arm. Neither of them were aware that the sun had set. Keenatay had built a fire in the shelter which provided light for them to work. *They are so focused and dedicated,* he thought. *And I am so grateful they're not giving up on this woman I love so dearly.*

When the bear had first grabbed Sabenta, the fierceness of his attack had dislocated her shoulder. The first thing they had to do was set it back in place.

"Keenatay, will you hold Sabenta very tightly to your chest so I can force her shoulder bones back to where they should be?" Maskanini asked. With tears in his eyes, Keenatay nodded and held her ever so close to him. He wondered if this was the last time the two of them would ever be this close again.

He heard and felt the bones of her shoulder snap back into place as Maskanini used all of his strength to reset them. Tears flowed down the cheeks of all three.

Next, they needed to repair the lacerations in her shoulder and arm. The torn tendons hung limply from where they had been attached.

Maskanini said, "Keenatay, cut some of your hair. I'll need long strands to reattach her tendons and muscles. And I'll need more light so I can see the wound better." Keenatay gladly gave Maskanini some of his hair, then held a burning piece of firewood closer to her shoulder wounds. Maskanini, with help from his ancient ancestors and a small bone needle, sewed the torn tendons back into their intended muscles. He also stitched several ripped muscles back together.

There were also deep gashes in Sabenta's side. Fortunately, she had no broken ribs. Maskanini mixed together the same ingredients Miantra and Sartaya had used for Nakia's wounds. Miantra held the girl's wounds open so her mate could spread the solution deep into the torn flesh, ensuring the infection fighting medicine was applied as deep as possible. Like Nakia's, these wounds would have to heal from the inside out. Therefore, they could not be sewn shut. These wounds would have to be constantly monitored and refreshed with the healing paste until they healed completely. The rest was up to the Great Spirit and Sabenta's will to live.

Miantra asked both men to bring her more fresh water so she could wash Sabenta's entire body to ensure there were no more wounds or injuries they would have to treat. And also to stave off any potential infection. While the men went for the water, Miantra carefully undressed the young woman and laid her bloodied clothes to the side. I'll wash these clothes tomorrow when the sun brings a new day, she thought. She then gently covered the young woman with a soft hide. When the men returned, Miantra thanked them and asked, "Will you ask several of the women from your tribe to help me bathe Sabenta?" The men nodded and turned to leave.

"I'll return to stay with you and Sabenta throughout the night," Maskanini added as he left the shelter with Keenatay.

Once the women had bathed her and determined she had no other wounds, they carefully lifted Sabenta's limp body onto half of a large elk hide and then folded the remaining half over her.

"I'll stay with her tonight in case she wakes up and needs some medicine to reduce her pain and to help her sleep," Miantra said to the women who had helped her. An older woman stated she would also stay in case Miantra needed her help in moving the young woman. The women's eyes met and they both smiled.

The next few nights would determine whether the young woman would live or not. The older woman with Miantra began humming a soothing tune and soon Miantra found herself humming right along with her. Throughout the night, the two women talked softly. Miantra learned the older woman was Sabenta's grandmother and her name was Wanectasii. She had raised Sabenta since she was twelve summers old. Wanectasii's daughter was the mother of Sabenta. She had died of a mysterious illness that had lasted for many full moons. Her daughter's mate was one of the better hunters and was gone often for long periods of time. As was tribal custom, Wanectasii assumed responsibility for her daughter's child after her daughter died.

Meanwhile, Keenatay and Maskanini joined the other men gathered around the Natayeh's large campfire. There was much commotion. Maskanini excused himself to see how his granddaughter and Nakia were doing. KiaNeeishtay motioned for Keenatay to join him. "I think it would be best if we paired up my men with your men around the perimeter of both camps. I don't want this bear sneaking up on any of our people and hurting anyone else. In the morning we'll gather our best trackers and hunters to find this bear and kill it."

"Agreed," said Keenatay. Together, the two leaders made plans for the hunt. The two men found solace in each other's company. They talked well into the early morning, sharing intimate details of their lives, forming a strong and unbreakable bond with one another.

In the meantime, Maskanini had walked over to his shelter to check on Nakia's condition. After assuring himself that Sartaya and Wakishtay had done everything possible to treat Nakia, he hugged his granddaughter tightly. "I'm so glad you weren't injured by the bear. You have done everything possible to help Nakia. I wouldn't have done anything differently. Now, I have to return to Sabenta's shelter. Thank you, Wakishtay, for helping Sartaya." He smiled at both of them as he left to rejoin his mate in caring for the severely injured woman.

Sartaya spent a fitful night drifting in and out of sleep. Resting next to Nakia, she'd been afraid of causing him more pain by rolling into him. From time to time she would stroke his head gently and whisper in his ears that she loved him. Nakia had not moved the entire night. When Sartaya did manage to sleep, she felt the presence of Nakia's mother but she couldn't see her. Sartaya prayed to both the mother of Nakia and the Great Spirit to save her brother and give him the strength he needed to survive. She thought she remembered somewhere in her dreams the blurred shape of a mountain lion running past her towards Nakia. She couldn't be certain because it happened so fast. *Maybe I just imagined it because I wanted it to happen so much.*

Wakishtay stayed with her the entire night. He, too, prayed to the Great Spirit to help Nakia and Sabenta survive. As dawn released its first rays of light, Wakishtay couldn't help but wonder about the bear attack that had caused all this pain. *I wonder why the bear fled, leaving the woman and Nakia on the ground. It could have easily carried either one of them away to . . . .* He shuddered, not wanting to complete that thought. *The spirits protected my granddaughter. How lucky she was. No. How fortunate we all were she wasn't a victim, too. If anything had happened to her I would rather . . . .* He pulled away from that thought, as well.

Now they were both awake and gazing into each other's eyes; one feeling sorrow and the other compassion. "Has Nakia moved at all during the night?" he asked his granddaughter.

"No, but I could hear him breathe, just barely. Oh Grandfather why did this have to happen? Why didn't the Great Spirit stop the attack? Where were our spirits? Why didn't they protect Sabenta and Nakia?" Brokenhearted, Sartaya slumped into her grandfather's waiting arms and cried inconsolably. The old man's tears fell softly down his weathered cheeks and onto her hair.

Once Sartaya's tears had dried she asked her grandfather, "Is Nakia going to die?" Wakishtay looked deep into her swollen red eyes.

"Granddaughter, only the Great Spirit knows whether your brother will live to hunt another day. If it is His wish, then He will breathe the necessary life back into Nakia. If the Great Spirit is lonely and wants Nakia for himself, then He will take him soon." Wakishtay continued, "But don't give up on Nakia just yet. Try to remember the visions all three of us have had because I believe they will yet happen. Nakia was right there with us in all of those visions. Sometimes, Sartaya, if we believe in something strong enough, it will come true."

"Oh, Grandfather, I do believe he will live. I believe it with all my heart," she cried earnestly.

Neither Maskanini, nor Miantra, nor Wanectasii, slept during the night. They constantly attended to cleaning the seeping wounds of the gravely injured young woman. The two women continued to hum throughout the night. Maskanini knew Sabenta would be in a death sleep for several days. It was the body's way of helping her. *But will she ever wake up?* he wondered. *If she lives, her shoulder will mend with time and be almost as good as it was before the attack. But all of her other wounds have turned purple and have become swollen.*

Throughout that dreadful night, Miantra repeatedly called upon the spirits of all her ancient ancestors who were medicine men and women to help Sabenta survive her wounds. *I dread the thought that Sartaya could have been attacked just as easily as this young woman was. We will need more medicine soon. I should go and get it before my mate needs it.* With that thought, she quickly rose and whispered into Maskanini's ear. He nodded gratefully and then turned his attention once again to the still form in front of him. Wanectasii continued to hum softly and occasionally stroked the young woman's cheek with her fingers.

When the first rays of sunlight appeared, the hunting group had already formed around the morning campfire. Everyone had eaten and was patiently awaiting daylight so they could begin the hunt. They were eager to put an end to this animal and to mount its head on a tribal pole for all to see. Hopefully, this gesture would help put everyone in both camps at ease.

Keenatay and KiaNeeishtay led the group of hunters out of the main camp and onto the trail leading toward the area where they found Nakia and Sabenta. It didn't take very long to reach the site of the attack. The leaders, with a motion of their hands, cautioned their men to be careful. No one had spoken a word, as silence was important if they wanted to surprise their prey.

The area where they had found Sabenta was covered with blood. They followed the trail of blood left by the bear for a short while until one of the trackers spotted the bear. He motioned to the men to quickly spread out to block any exit the bear might try to use when it realized the danger it was in.

As they eased closer to the creature, it appeared the bear was asleep, nestled between a large fallen log and a clutter of dead branches. As they got even closer, the bear never stirred. Keenatay was close enough now to throw his spear with deadly accuracy. Just as he was ready to throw, KiaNeeishtay raised his hand.

"The bear isn't breathing. I think that it's already dead." Both Keenatay and KiaNeeishtay, tense and wary, crept up to the huge black bear ready to drive their spears into its chest if they detected even the slightest movement. Once close enough, they both prodded the bear with their spears. Nothing happened. The creature didn't flinch. It was dead.

All the hunters gathered around and stared at the bear in amazement. Its head rested on its dried, blood-matted chest. When several of the men raised the bear's head they noticed the wood splinters from two arrow shafts that were deeply imbedded in the bear's throat. As they all crowded closer, they saw that one of the arrows had severed one of the bear's neck arteries. "How could that be? Whose arrows are they?" asked one of the hunters.

KiaNeeishtay looked closer at the broken shafts of wood and recognized the unique markings. "They belong to a member of our tribe," he replied. Several of his tribesmen took a closer look and also recognized the markings as belonging to one very special member of the Natayeh. They smiled and were about to mention the person's name when KiaNeeishtay gave them a quick glance, warning them not to say anything more.

"I will bring the slayer of the bear to our next campfire for all of you to meet. Until then, we should gut this rogue bear and haul it back to camp for all to see. Once everyone sees it's dead, they will no longer fear for their lives."

As the men went about the task of removing the bear's entrails, Keenatay tried to imagine the events that took place during the savage attack on the beautiful woman he planned to take as his mate. *What exactly happened here? How did she escape? The wolf . . . What happened to the wolf and what part did it play in saving Sabenta? I wonder if it will survive. Sabenta was injured so badly. I cannot bear the thought of losing her. Will we ever be together again in this life? Her fate is in the Great Spirit's hands now.* As he helped with the bear, he wondered, *Who was the brave hunter of the Natayeh to fell this bear with his arrows? And why didn't he mention his kill to anyone else? I'll speak with KiaNeeishtay about this. We should honor this man for trying to save Sabenta. I will embrace this man in front of both tribes and personally thank him for his courage.*

"KiaNeeishtay, I must return to camp to be with Sabenta. Please, come see me this evening. I want to know more about this brave hunter who killed the bear." Having spoken to the leader of the other tribe, he sprinted back to camp, praying to the Great Spirit to help the love of his life to survive her wounds.

The men from both tribes made quick work of gutting the animal that had turned the lives of their tribes upside down. Then, they tied the bear to six strong branches they had found close to where the bear had taken its last breath. Four branches, spaced one arm length apart, were tied to the bear length-wise. The other two branches were somewhat shorter and tied underneath the ends of the four branches about an arm length in from their tips. This allowed up to eight men to help carry the heavy weight of the carcass. It would have been much easier if they had butchered the bear into pieces. But both Keenatay and KiaNeeishtay had agreed that the entire bear should be brought back to camp. The people of both tribes needed to see the huge dead beast for themselves.

CHAPTER 26

There was much commotion at the edge of the Natayeh's campsite when the hunters appeared carrying the carcass of the large bear. Members of both tribes shouted and howled as they gathered around the hunters and their dead quarry. The hunters propped the bear up on the carrying poles near the Natayeh's main campfire so everyone could see just how large and fierce the animal was. Some of the women and many of the children shrieked at the sight. The men stood in awe as they tried to imagine the attack that took place on Sabenta. *How could anyone have survived such an attack by this beast?* They all wondered.

After most members of each tribe had seen the spectacle the Natayeh leader instructed the hunters to skin the animal and butcher the meat into equal parcels for both tribes. The bear's hide was then stretched out, tied, and mounted onto branches anchored in the ground by the campfire. Its head was cut from the rest of the usable hide, then stuck on a tall pole and placed so that it was just above the drying hide. It created an awesome sight and proved even more fearsome at night when the roaring campfire highlighted the bear's features.

KiaNeeishtay headed over to the Zakenaque's camp. He wanted to join Keenatay who was already with Sabenta. He announced his presence at the opening to her shelter, not wanting to enter unless he was invited in by Keenatay.

"Come in," Keenatay said, his voice filled with anguish. As KiaNeeishtay entered, his gaze met the glistening eyes of his counterpart who knelt beside the woman he loved. Only then did KiaNeeishtay look down at the woman. Maskanini and Miantra kept wiping her wounds clean as they seeped a reddish, green and yellow discharge.

Maskanini said quietly, "She hasn't awakened yet and I don't expect her to for several more days." *If she does at all*, he thought to himself. Sabenta's grandmother hummed a gentle melody while caressing her granddaughter's head which rested on her lap.

"There will be a campfire tonight so that everything that's happened in the last day and a half can be explained to everyone. Will you join me tonight?" KiaNeeishtay asked Keenatay.

"Yes. I'll join you later. For now, I want to stay with Sabenta." KiaNeeishtay nodded and began to leave. "Oh, will the hunter that shot the bear be there so I can personally thank him?"

"All will be revealed tonight," KiaNeeishtay said as he left the shelter and headed for his tribe's camp. *There are going to be some very surprised people at tonight's campfire. For now, I must talk with Sartaya.*

Sartaya and her grandfather were still kneeling beside Nakia when KiaNeeishtay arrived at Maskanini's shelter and asked if he could enter.

"Please come in," Wakishtay said. "How is Sabenta?" he asked, trusting that KiaNeeishtay would have already stopped at her shelter when he returned from the bear hunt.

"She continues in a death sleep, much like Nakia. The next couple of days will see if she lives or dies. It's up to the Great Spirit now. How badly is Nakia injured?" he asked looking at both of them.

Sartaya's eyes filled with tears as her grandfather answered. "He has many broken ribs and deep wounds from the bear's powerful claws. Sartaya and I reset his ribs and applied medicine. It may be days before we know anything. Where did you find the bear?" the old hunter asked. He had known from the amount of blood leading away from the attack area that the bear had been mortally wounded. But he'd said nothing as he quickly returned to camp with Sartaya and her severely injured wolf brother.

"We found the bear resting against a large fallen log a little ways from the attack site. It was already dead. When we raised its head, we saw pieces of two arrows sticking out from its throat. One of them had severed an artery and the bear bled to death." He paused and looked directly at the young girl. "Sartaya, those arrows were yours."

Silence filled the shelter as the two men waited for Sartaya's response.

"I forgot I shot two arrows into the bear." Her eyes opened wide and filled with horror as she remembered what had happened. "Everything happened so fast. I saw the bear dragging Sabenta away as if she were nothing . . . but then it dropped her when Nakia ran in front of it. He jumped onto the bear and tried to bite its neck and the bear flung him against the tree trunk and I heard his ribs . . . . Nakia was slumped over at the base of the tree, not making a sound.

"When the bear returned for Sabenta I shot an arrow in its throat. That only made the bear angrier. He stood up, but I don't think he saw me in the high grass. Just as he turned in my direction, I shot a second arrow. This time, a lot of blood spurted from his wound. He must have gotten scared with all the blood he was losing, because he turned and walked away kind of wobbly. I was so scared he would come back, but I vowed not to leave the woman's side until the others arrived.

"She was so badly hurt. If the bear had come back . . . ." Sartaya shuddered. "I don't know what would have happened. Then I went to Nakia. He was so still and not making a sound. I thought he was dead. Grandfather, he attacked the bear and made it drop Sabenta. I caught up to him just as the bear dropped her, and threw him against the tree trunk. I heard his ribs crack. It was a terrible sound and Nakia cried out and slumped to the ground. Oh, Grandfather, it was horrible!" Both men had to catch their breath. *No child should ever have to go through this kind of experience,* they thought.

Except for Maskanini, Miantra, and Wanectasii, almost everyone in both camps attended the evening campfire. Wakishtay and Sartaya stayed with Nakia.

Many from both tribes gazed up at the head of the bear on top of the pole, positioned just above the animal's outstretched hide. The large campfire cast bright flickers of light onto the huge form, making it appear even more ferocious and almost alive. Many shuddered at the thought of this huge beast attacking them. It was an awesome and fearful sight.

Keenatay made his way over to KiaNeeishtay and held out his right arm. KiaNeeishtay grasped the other tribal leader's forearm, completing the half circles given to each of them by Maskanini during the welcoming ceremony. The two men's eyes met. As everyone settled on the ground around the large campfire, the leader of the Natayeh remained standing. The crowd became silent as he lifted his hands.

"Yesterday, something horrific happened to several of our loved ones." This statement caused some confusion among the tribal guests as they had heard only one person was attacked. "While Sabenta was out gathering food with several other women, she was viciously attacked by this large black bear. When the bear grabbed her shoulder in his huge jaws and began dragging her away, Sartaya and Nakia heard her screams and ran to help her. Nakia leapt at the huge bear, trying to bury his fangs in the bear's throat. Well, as all of you can see, this was a very large bear and most of you have by now seen Nakia, so you know that he was no match for this beast.

"The bear was unharmed but very annoyed by his much smaller attacker. It dropped Sabenta so it could use its long claws to slash at Nakia. It then flung the wolf's body against a tree, breaking many of Nakia's ribs. With his many injuries, Nakia may not survive this night. Sartaya and Wakishtay are now by his side tending to his wounds. The bear then returned to Sabenta to grab her again and drag her away." Keenatay grimaced at the scene already seared into his mind. Everyone else listened in horror, staring at the terrifying beast that seemed to glare and lunge toward them as the flames danced in the roaring campfire.

The Natayeh leader then asked Keenatay if he would share what he and the hunters had found earlier in the morning when they went after the bear to kill it. Keenatay nodded, now guessing who might have shot the arrows that killed the bear, but having a difficult time believing it.

"Last night we posted men around the perimeter of our two camps in case the bear returned to attack us. Neither KiaNeeishtay nor I wanted to take any chances after this bear had already attacked one of us. Ah, I'm sorry, I meant to say attacked two of us, Sabenta and

Nakia." KiaNeeishtay appreciated his thoughtfulness in remembering that Nakia was truly a member of the Natayeh. "Fortunately, the bear did not approach our camps last night."

Keenatay looked up at the menacing form of the bear, shook his head in disgust, and continued. "At first light this morning, a group of trackers and hunters from both of our tribes set out to track this animal down and kill it. When we arrived at the scene of the attack on Sabenta and Nakia, we saw blood everywhere. We thought all of the blood belonged to Sabenta and the wolf. But then we found even more blood leading away from the attack site. We wondered if there had been another victim.

"We quickly followed this trail of blood and spotted the bear a little ways from where the attack took place. It seemed to be sleeping against a large fallen log among a bunch of dead branches. KiaNeeishtay and I crept up with our spears ready to throw. As we got closer, I was ready to thrust my spear into the bear's heart, but KiaNeeishtay motioned for me to wait. We both moved a little closer and finally jabbed our spears at the bear's chest. It didn't move. The bear was dead. 'How could this be?' we all wondered.

"This is the part that gets really interesting," he continued. "Several of our hunters lifted the bear's head and discovered several broken arrow shafts imbedded in the bear's neck. It had been shot twice. One of the arrows had severed a main blood vessel. That's why there was so much blood leading away from the attack area. I didn't recognize the markings on the arrow shafts, but KiaNeeishtay did. He didn't want to tell me then who had shot those arrows that caused the bear to run away. I believe he would now like to share with all of us who that courageous person was." Having said that, Keenatay nodded to the leader of the Natayeh and sat down.

"Sartaya, the Granddaughter of our Maskanini and Miantra, had arrived just in time to see the bear drop Sabenta and throw Nakia against the tree trunk. She heard his piercing cry as his ribs cracked like so many wooden sticks. I know that many of you from the Zakenaque may find what I am about to tell you hard to believe. You see, in our tribe, we train all of our children, including our daughters, how to track and to hunt at a young age."

This caused much commotion among the visiting tribal members, because in all their travels, among all the different tribes that they had visited, none had displayed this custom. KiaNeeishtay paused briefly to let his guests think about what he had just shared with them. Then he raised his hands once again. The crowd fell silent out of custom and respect for their hosting tribe's leader.

KiaNeeishtay wondered how the visiting tribe was going to react to what he was about to tell them. "As Sartaya came upon this grisly scene, the bear stood straight up, stealing one last look at the wolf's body slumped down at the bottom of the tree where he had flung him moments ago. Just as the bear turned to grab the young woman with its huge powerful jaws, an arrow pierced the back of its neck and protruded out the front. The bear jerked upward and roared in pain and anger. Tasting some of his own blood, he turned, in rage, to see what had attacked him. Another arrow flew into the front side of his throat, only this time it severed one of his main neck arteries. Now the amount of blood he was swallowing was choking him. Blood also spurted out from his neck wound. He sensed he was in real danger and turned to flee. His legs wouldn't carry him as fast as he would have liked to run, but he did manage to wobble away on all fours, coughing and spitting out blood from his mouth in great quantities." By now, everyone from the visiting tribe wondered who had shot the arrows.

KiaNeeishtay continued, "Sartaya was afraid the bear would return, but put her fears aside and ran over to comfort the young woman who was unconscious. Her wounds were deep and ugly. Sartaya didn't want to scream for help, fearing the bear would hear her and return to finish them all off.

"The other women Sabenta had been with earlier heard the terrible sounds of the attack and raced back to where they had left her. When they arrived, they were horrified by what they saw. Sabenta's Grandmother, Wanectasii, stayed with her and instructed the others to run back to camp for help. Sartaya, whose clothes were all bloody from holding the young woman's ravaged body in her arms went over to Nakia's broken body. This is what we saw when we arrived from camp."

KiaNeeishtay now looked directly into Keenatay's glistening eyes. "Sartaya shot those arrows into the beast that attacked the woman you love. Her quick action and accuracy is what drove the fierce bear away. You see, Sartaya has been trained to track and to hunt by her grandfather, Wakishtay, who is the greatest tracker and hunter our tribe has ever known. He could still outtrack and outhunt any of our younger men, if his aching old body would only let him." KiaNeeishtay paused to observe the many nodding heads and knowing smiles of his own proud people who surrounded him. "Now, he provides an equally important service to our people. He shares his skills with our younger children, both boys and girls, so both can track and hunt as they grow into young men and women. For many generations this has been the custom of our people.

"Nakia was the first to attack the bear, causing it to drop Sabenta. In doing so, he was injured severely and may not live through the night. This is what truly happened. Now, I must go and visit Sartaya and Nakia. I will ask the Great Spirit to save both Sabenta and Nakia." Having said that, KiaNeeishtay headed toward the shelter where Sartaya, Wakishtay, and Nakia were. Everyone else understood that the meeting was over when the Natayeh Leader left.

Keenatay headed toward the shelter where Sabenta was being cared for. Every man, woman, and child at the campfire was mesmerized by what they had just heard.

The Zakenaque guests had a hard time believing that a young girl had shot and killed this large and ferocious bear. They still had a hard time understanding she had a wolf for a brother, and that he had probably saved Sabenta's life. Some, though, were beginning to feel sorrow for the wolf. The Natayeh tribal members, though very worried about the severe injuries Sabenta and the wolf had suffered, could not have been more proud of Sartaya and Nakia.

As the campfire burned down to just a glow, the area around it was mostly empty, except for the grotesque shape of the bear looming above it. Many of those who had been there from the beginning of the night had left without saying a word. The majority of the shelters for both tribes were unusually quiet for this time of night. People lay down to sleep, but their eyes would not close. If they did, horrifying images of the bear attack replayed over and over in their minds.

Everyone slept late the next morning, except for a few babies wanting to be cleaned and fed. Keenatay admired the persistence of Maskanini and his mate, Miantra. Neither one had rested in nearly two days of tending to the injured Sabenta. *I will never forget their dedication to the woman I love,* he vowed. *This tribe, these Natayeh . . . there are many things we can learn from them and take back to the Smokey Mountains; things that will make us better.* He made a promise he would repay the kindness of this tribe, especially Sartaya and Nakia, and Maskanini and his mate, Miantra.

That evening Keenatay visited Maskanini's shelter. He announced himself and Wakishtay gave him permission to enter.

"Sartaya, how is Nakia?" he asked.

"He sleeps most of the time. His injuries were very severe. I don't know whether he'll live through another night," she answered, tears trickling down her smooth cheeks.

"He was very brave to attack a beast as large as that bear. You were also very brave, Sartaya, to shoot the bear. You and Nakia saved Sabenta from a fate worse than anything I want to imagine. Whatever the Great Spirit decides, I'll always be indebted to you. I've been asking the Great Spirit to spare both Sabenta and Nakia. Just as Nakia means a lot to you, Sabenta means everything to me. She is to be my mate," he choked. Sartaya embraced him.

"How is Sabenta?" Wakishtay asked, wiping moisture from his eyes.

"Also sleeping. I don't know whether she will live to see another sunrise. I must return to her side now." The Zakenaque leader looked deep into Sartaya's eyes before he left. "Thank you again, Sartaya, for risking your life to save the woman that I care for more than life itself."

After several days, Sabenta, although not awake, was taking a special broth prepared by Maskanini and his mate. At first, it was difficult to even get her mouth open, but after much persistence Miantra was able to feed the young woman. They knew that a milestone had been reached when her reflexive swallowing kicked in. *The Great Spirit wants this woman to live!*

Keenatay stayed by her side, helping in every way he could. He took turns cleansing her wounds and helping her drink the special, life-sustaining broth. He held her hand and whispered to her all the things that were going on in camp. When he wasn't by her side, he tended to the day-to-day needs of his tribe. His people knew what he was going through and, for the most part, took care of their own needs. For this, he was both grateful and proud of his people.

Nakia also began to slowly recover, making a little progress with each new day. Although every breath was painful, he took in the life-sustaining fluids Sartaya had prepared for him. Once in a while, he would open his eyes as if to say thank you, then fall back into a deep sleep. While he slept, his spirit traveled great distances at his mother's side. She was with him every moment since the bear attack on the young woman. She had watched when he leapt at the bear. She was very proud of Nakia's courage. While his body slept, his mother filled his spirit with her love and experience. *The Great Spirit wants Nakia to survive. His destiny is to walk with his sister and protect her as she continues her journey through life.*

CHAPTER 27

A few days after the bear attack, Keenatay approached KiaNeeishtay and asked, "May I take the bear's hide and prepare it as a gift to Sartaya? I want to show her how grateful I am for her courage in saving Sabenta's life."

"Of course. How is Sabenta?"

"Each new day, she takes a little more of the special broth they've prepared for her. But she still sleeps. I don't know if she'll ever wake up. Your Maskanini and his mate are wonderful and caring people. They haven't left her side since the attack. Everyone has been very helpful to me and my people since we arrived at your camp. Every day, someone from your tribe has brought food over to Sabenta's shelter and they have promised to ask the Great Spirit for His help in healing her. I hope someday I'll be able to repay all of you for your kindness. Has Nakia improved at all?"

"Yes. He, too, drinks small portions of the broth prepared by Sartaya. He still sleeps most of the day, as well."

"Sartaya prepared his special medicine broth?"

KiaNeeishtay hesitated, unsure of just how much information to share with Keenatay about Sartaya's skills as a medicine woman. *Will he understand? Yes,* KiaNeeishtay decided, *he's a very capable leader.*

"Wakishtay has been helping Sartaya to treat Nakia," the Natayeh leader said. "You may find what I am about to tell you a little difficult to understand. Sometimes, even I'm surprised and have a hard time understanding the things this girl of only thirteen summers is capable of doing."

Keenatay smiled and said, “I have noticed things about this young girl who is only thirteen summers old. She has a wolf for a brother. She wears a bracelet made from the claws of an adult wolf. She carries a knife, a bow, and quiver of arrows. She also carries a beautifully carved spear with the image of a mountain lion being killed. She wears a necklace of claws from a mountain lion. Several days ago she saved the love of my life by killing a ferocious bear with two of her arrows that she makes herself. What is there not to understand?” he asked. “Now, it seems, you are about to tell me something else about this remarkable girl.”

KiaNeeishtay smiled. “I knew you would understand.” The two men enjoyed laughing for the first time since the bear attack. After regaining his composure, the Natayeh leader continued, “Several full moons ago, Maskanini told me that all of the Natayeh’s ancient ancestors, who were our medicine men and medicine women throughout all of time, had visited Sartaya and her grandmother in a Dream Vision. During their visit, they instilled their combined knowledge of medicine and healing into Sartaya’s spirit. It was their decision for her to become the youngest medicine woman in the history of our tribe. So yes, besides everything else you have observed about her, Sartaya is also a medicine woman.

“As it turned out, the timing for this was good. With both Maskanini and Miantra needing to be at Sabenta’s side, Sartaya could treat Nakia herself. Otherwise, our brother Nakia most certainly would have died. Throughout the past winter, spring, and early part of this summer, before your tribe arrived, most of my people have seen Sartaya helping Maskanini and Miantra to treat the sick. She’s become very skilled in a very short period of time. Even though she’s very young, we all have confidence in her capabilities.”

Keenatay sat deep in thought for a long moment. “Why do you think this child has been given all of these special abilities at such an early age?”

“I don’t know. No one seems to know,” KiaNeeishtay replied. “Most of us do agree that the Great Spirit has placed her in our tribe at this point in time for something very important. She has wisdom beyond her age. She is fearless and has great courage. She cares for and looks out for everyone else. She is a teacher to both the young and old of things that really matter. Sartaya has a wolf for a brother and is now a medicine woman. Her destiny is not for us to decide. It's already been written by the Ancients who are guided by the Great Spirit."

"Your tribe is very fortunate to have not only a Maskanini, but two medicine women as well," Keenatay commented. "We recently lost our Maskanini to a strange illness even he couldn't overcome. He often talked about training someone to become a Maskanini or medicine woman. He had no mate or children. The last time I approached him about it, he said he hadn't yet found the right person. We thought time was on our side, but the Great Spirit must have needed him more than we did. Now, we are without anyone who understands medicine. I have visited other tribes looking for a Maskanini or medicine woman who might be able to help us, but none could spare who they had." Keenatay understood that Maskanini and Miantra were too old to travel to the Zakenaque's homeland even if they wanted to help. He also realized Sartaya would become the Natayeh's Medicine Woman once her grandparents were too old to perform that function.

KiaNeeishtay could guess what Keenatay was thinking. *There's no one to take care of his people's ailments. The Natayeh have been fortunate for many generations to always have at least one person who could heal our sick and broken.* "I will ask the Great Spirit to help you find a Maskanini or medicine woman. I can't imagine what would have happened if we had no one to care for Sabenta after that vicious bear attack."

"Thank you, KiaNeeishtay. I'll leave this problem in the hands of the Great Spirit. There's nothing more that I can do about it at the moment."

KiaNeeishtay wanted to change the subject to something lighter. "Keenatay, would you walk with me to where we planned on holding the games and contests over the next two full moons?"

Keenatay understood exactly what his new friend meant. He nodded. "People will have to practice for them over the next fourteen days. The distraction will be good for them. What kinds of contests would your people like?"

"Why don't you explain one of your favorites to me, and then I'll describe one of mine. After all, you are my guest," KiaNeeishtay countered.

Keenatay thought for a moment. "The Hoop and Spear game is very popular with my people. Have your people ever played it?"

"Yes, we learned it the last time we visited you. We've played it here ever since. My people really enjoy it."

"The Hoop and Spear game is my idea. What contest do you suggest?"

"Have you ever played Shinny?"

"I've not heard of it," Keenatay responded.

The two men spent most of the afternoon choosing the rest of the games and contests their people would be participating in. They identified games for just men to play, for just women and some just for children. There were contests meant for individuals and for teams. It promised to be an exciting time for both tribes. By the time they finished deciding, they were both ready for the evening meal and headed back to their shelters.

CHAPTER 28

Sabenta awoke from her death sleep five days after the attack and was able to take her medicine and healing broth regularly. Her shoulder still hurt very much, but the repairs performed by Maskanini and Miantra seemed to be taking hold. The medicines applied to her wounds kept them free from infections.

Although Sabenta was still in great pain, she smiled often to those caring for her. Her face especially lit up whenever Keenatay visited. He came several times a day so Maskanini and his mate could return to their shelter and rest, as well as check up on Nakia's progress. Wanectasii also relieved the older couple whenever they needed to take a break.

Whenever Keenatay visited his intended mate, they held hands and talked about their future. She adored everything about him, and he loved her more than life itself. "I'm hoping I can watch some of the games and contests," she said. "How are you getting along with the Natayeh leader?"

"I have great respect for KiaNeeishtay. He and I have become brothers. He stopped by each day you were sleeping after the attack."

"Maskanini and Miantra saved my life with their knowledge of medicine, didn't they?" she asked.

"Yes, they didn't leave your side for days while your spirit struggled to stay alive."

"When I was sleeping so deeply, I had many visions. I also remember every word you whispered to me when you thought I wasn't listening," she said, blushing. His face reddened with surprise. "One vision I had over and over was of a large beautiful wolf. I believe it was the mother of Sartaya's wolf brother. I don't know how I know this, I just do. Did her brother somehow help me?"

Keenatay looked deep into Sabenta's eyes as he searched for the right words. "Nakia and Sartaya saved your life. Nakia jumped on the bear, causing it to drop you. The bear almost killed him, but Nakia is slowly healing. Sartaya shot two arrows into the bear's neck and he stumbled away, then bled to death. Once the bear left, Sartaya ran to your side and held you. She's the bravest little girl I have ever known."

"Who is taking care of Nakia if Maskanini and Miantra arc caring for me?"

"Sartaya, with Wakishtay's help. This is hard to believe, but Sartaya is also a medicine woman. Just before the attack occurred, the Natayeh's ancient healers visited Sartaya in a Dream Vision. They shared with her spirit all their knowledge of medicine and healing and who knows what else. If they hadn't chosen to make her a medicine woman at that time, Nakia would most certainly have joined his mother in the spirit world."

"The Great Spirit must have many plans for them; just as He must have great plans for you and me," she said with a confident smile. "I'm tired. Will you stay with me until I fall asleep?" She didn't wait for him to answer, just closed her eyes and drifted off to sleep.

Keenatay knew she would heal and be alright. Her condition did concern him though, as he considered the long and arduous return trip home. *Sabenta will never be healed in time for when we must begin our long journey back,* he concluded. *I don't want to leave without her. I almost lost her. I don't want to be without her ever again. But she'll be in no condition to join us. I must talk with KiaNeeishtay. I'll have to depend on his people to care for her until she's well enough to travel. But how will she rejoin us in the Smokey Mountains? She can't go alone. Who of this tribe will want to make such a long trip? I'll ask the Great Spirit for guidance. For now, I just want to gaze upon her while she sleeps.*

Maskanini and Miantra were always grateful when Keenatay relieved them and they could return to their own shelter to check on Nakia. Today was no exception. "How is Nakia today?" Miantra asked Sartaya.

"Still weak, even though he's been taking the healing broth several times a day he still doesn't seem to have much energy. He won't take any of the meat we've tried to give him. Wakishtay and I have been keeping his wounds clean with the medicine paste. The gashes seem to be healing slowly from the inside out."

"Have you tried giving him more of the medicine to relieve his pain? He may be reluctant to stand because of the pain he's still feeling," Maskanini added. "Once he begins to stand and walk around, he'll probably begin to take some small pieces of meat. Then he can gain his strength more quickly. Each day, encourage him to stand and take a few steps."

"I'll do that, Grandfather. How is Sabenta? Is she improving?"

"She gets better with each new day. She may even be able to sit up in another seven days. Keenatay is with her now. Your grandmother and I will return after we've had our evening meal. Is anyone else hungry?"

"We've all been invited to share a meal with Lakato and his family. They're waiting for us now," Wakishtay responded. "Sartaya, I know you want to stay with Nakia, so I'll bring some food back with me when I return."

"Thank you, Grandfather. Maybe Yukawe will bring me some food if you ask him to. That way you can visit longer with Lakato. I've missed talking with Yukawe while I've been caring for Nakia."

Wakishtay nodded and reminded himself to make sure Sartaya took a break tomorrow from caring for Nakia and play with her friends. *She hasn't left his side since the bear attack.*

Maskanini, Miantra, and Wakishtay left to join Lakato and Bosaata for their evening meal. Wakishtay didn't have to suggest to Yukawe to take Sartaya some food. Yukawe beat him to it and suggested he take enough food to her shelter for the both of them.

"They both really seem to enjoy each other's company," Lakato said after his son had left. Everyone nodded in agreement.

"Sartaya, it's Yukawe. May I come in? I have some food for us."

Sartaya was delighted to see her friend. "Yes, please. I'm so glad to see you. I didn't realize how hungry I was until I smelled the food you brought."

Yukawe put the bowl of food on some stone slabs between them, then sat down. "How is Nakia?"

"He is doing better each day. He hasn't stood up yet, but I think I'll encourage him to stand tomorrow. Maybe if he stands, he'll take some small pieces of meat. Grandfather says he'll get stronger once he can eat meat again. He was hurt so badly by the bear. Oh, Yukawe, I thought I had lost him," she said softly.

"I could help you with Nakia. Together, we could raise him up to stand on his feet several times a day, as long as Wakishtay wouldn't mind. I've been worried about you both ever since that horrible day."

"I don't think my grandfather would mind. I know he has many other things to do, but he hasn't left me alone with Nakia since the attack. He helped me set Nakia's broken ribs and turned him whenever I needed to treat his wounds with medicine paste. He loves Nakia very much." The tears ran down her cheeks as she imagined the pain Nakia must have felt.

"Please ask him if it would be alright for me to help you. I don't want to offend him. He's become like a grandfather to me this past summer. I've really appreciated him asking me to go with him and Nakia to hunt while you've been with your grandmother. He's taught me much."

Yukawe paused and then gently held her hands in his. He looked deep into her eyes and said, "Sartaya, you were very brave to kill that bear. You saved Nakia and Sabenta from a horrible death. When I first heard about the bear attack, I asked the Great Spirit to protect you from all harm. Then, when I heard about Nakia's and Sabenta's injuries, I felt bad that I didn't ask the Great Spirit to protect them as well. Now I ask the Great Spirit to heal them both. Sartaya, do you want to talk about it with me? After all, we did survive a mountain lion attack together."

She smiled at him, sensing his compassion for her. "It's been hard not to think about it. I lay wide awake most nights, seeing Nakia crushed and thrown against the tree trunk by that huge bear. I hear his ribs crack. And I'll never forget Sabenta caught in the jaws of that beast. Her arm was nearly torn off her shoulder. I keep wondering how either one of them survived such an attack. Yet, they both live."

"Yes, because you shot that bear with your arrows. You saved them. Though I wonder what made you decide to shoot the bear in his throat."

"At the time, I didn't really think about it. I sensed Nakia's mother there. Her spirit seemed to leap at the bear's throat. But now that I've had time to think about it, I don't think my bow could have wounded the bear anywhere else but in his throat. I was going to shoot a third arrow, but the bear seemed scared and staggered away from us. I didn't know he was dead until KiaNeeishtay stopped by our shelter to ask how Nakia was. I'd forgotten I'd shot the bear until he asked me about the two arrows they'd found in the bear's throat. I hope I can sleep tonight."

"Maybe by talking about it, you'll start to feel better," Yukawe suggested. "In eleven days, the two tribes will be competing in games and contests. Let's try to help Nakia get strong enough to watch them with us. Even if we have to carry him, he can still be with us. Maybe Sabenta will also be able to watch some of the events. If she does, we can sit Nakia beside her. I'm sure she'd love to have him and you sit next to her. It will be great fun for all of us."

"I'm beginning to feel better already. You're a good friend, Yukawe. I'll mention to my grandparents that we want to bring Nakia to some of the games and contests."

"If you're finished eating, I'll leave what's left for you. I should let you rest." He reached for her hands and held them tightly in his while looking directly into her eyes. "It was nice to see you again, Sartaya. Thank you for sharing with me what really happened during the attack. I think you will sleep better tonight," he said with a reassuring smile as he left her shelter.

She watched him as he left, then thought, "He's truly a wonderful friend. But what are these other feelings I seem to have for him, especially when he held my hands? I've never felt like this before."

Sartaya knelt closer to Nakia and gently brushed his head with her hand. "Did you hear that, Nakia? You're coming with us to watch some of the games and contests. That means you'll have to get stronger. Tomorrow, Yukawe and I will help you stand and maybe even take a few steps. Once you can stand and take a few steps, I promise we'll give you some of your favorite meat to eat." *Did Nakia's eyes just become more alert or am I imagining it? I'll speak to Wakishtay about Yukawe's suggestion.*

CHAPTER 29

Wakishtay agreed to let Yukawe help Sartaya take care of Nakia. *There's still so much to do to prepare for the coming events,* Wakishtay thought. *But I'll still visit Sartaya each day to check on Nakia's progress. I'm glad Yukawe will be helping her. They're good for each other. Maybe Nakia will be able to sit for awhile and watch the contests. That would be wonderful.*

The next morning following breakfast, Yukawe went over to Sartaya's shelter to help her with Nakia. "Sartaya, can I help you lift Nakia up and see if he'll walk with us for a few steps? We can give him some meat as a reward if he does."

"Yes. Why don't you stand outside the shelter by our campfire with some pieces of raw meat in your hands? That's far enough. Now, call to him and offer him the meat."

"Come here, Nakia. I have some meat for you. See?" Nakia hurt with each step he took. But he was very hungry, so he eased towards Yukawe. When he reached him, he thoroughly enjoyed his reward. Both Sartaya and Yukawe were elated with the number of steps the wolf took. "Tomorrow, we'll encourage him to walk even further," Yukawe suggested.

Each day, while the victims healed, members of both tribes spent as much time as they could preparing themselves for the games and contests. Even Keenatay was excited about some of the contests, especially when it had to do with spear throwing. *I think I'll surprise our hosts when it comes time to see who can throw a spear the furthest with accuracy. Lakato will be delighted with what I have to show him.*

Time passed quickly. The day arrived for the games and contests to begin. Sabenta could now sit upright and watch her tribe compete with the Natayeh. Nakia could stand and walk a short distance. He enjoyed the fresh meat Sartaya and Yukawe gave him as a reward for his efforts.

Sabenta was carried out to the edge of the contest field the first day of the games. An improvised chair allowed her to sit upright so she could watch the competitions. Nakia was also carried out to the field on a makeshift stretcher by Sartaya and Yukawe. They set the wolf down next to Sabenta who appreciated the gesture. She laid her good hand on Nakia's forehead. "Thank you, Nakia, for saving my life at the risk of your own." He looked up at her and licked her hand.

"Sartaya, would you come closer to me for a moment?" This was the first time since that horrible day that either of them had seen each other. Sartaya knelt down in front of Sabenta. The injured woman held her good hand out and smiled warmly. Sartaya clasped the woman's hand in both of hers. When they touched, emotions surged up and filled both of them to overflowing. Tears cascaded down both their cheeks. Sartaya wanted to embrace her, but was afraid she might cause her more pain. Sabenta wanted to embrace Sartaya, but couldn't because of her still healing shoulder.

"Sartaya, if not for you, I wouldn't be here now. Your courage, without any concern for yourself, saved my life. I'll always be indebted to you for this gift of life. Now, let's watch the fun together, shall we?" Sartaya blushed and nodded in agreement, then sat down next to the injured woman. "Who is that next to you, Sartaya?"

"Yukawe. He is my close friend who's been helping me take care of Nakia."

Sabenta smiled at the boy and pointing at herself said, "I am Sabenta and happy to be alive, thanks to your friend, Sartaya." Yukawe beamed with pride for his friend. He nodded in acknowledgement of Sabenta and sat down next to Nakia. The injured woman made a mental note of the mountain lion claws strung around each of their necks. *There is surely an interesting story here. I'll have to remember to ask them about their necklaces. Why would children be wearing the claws of a mountain lion?*

The first game played was Hoop and Spear, played by two men

with multi-colored wood tipped spears. The game tested fleetness, eyesight, and skill in throwing. One man carrying a spear would roll a hoop laced with a multi-colored rawhide. Then both men would throw their spears into the multi-colored rawhide to try and stop the hoop from rolling. The colors on the spears and on the hoops counted for different points. Men from both tribes were paired off. After awhile, it was clear the Zakenaque had played this game often. They had more high scores than the Natayeh.

The second game was called Shinny. This game was played with sticks that had curved and cupped ends which held a small ball. Two posts or stakes set three paces apart at the ends of the field served as goals. Any number of players could be on a team. The Natayeh, who had played Shinny for dozens of summers, dominated this game

Each of the games was played for several days so that each tribe could better understand how the games should be played. The end results were similar for each of the games, but each tribe greatly enjoyed themselves. These and other games went on for many days. Everyone enjoyed themselves. Sabenta was able to watch the games each day for short periods of time before she tired and needed to be carried back to her shelter. Nakia was by her side until she had to leave. Usually, when she left the field, he was also carried back to Sartaya's shelter to rest.

There were many victory feasts and many huge campfires where the winning teams were given much latitude in describing how they had won that day. A lot of teasing and laughter went on among the contestants, as well as those who had watched the games. Even though the bear attack still lingered in everyone's minds, they tried their best to get past it.

After these events ended, contests of skill using bows and arrows and spears began. Eleven grass figures of familiar animals and large birds were strategically placed throughout the contest field. Each target had a different distance from which the participants had to shoot. The targets had different colored circles painted on strategic areas, indicating actual kill spots. Each colored circle represented a good, better, or best accuracy value. Usually two men, one from each tribe, were paired up to shoot at each of the grass targets. Once they'd both shot at the last target, two more men would begin the course. By the end of the third day, all of the men had finished the course. The two tribes were evenly matched.

Now it was the women's turn. Since none of the visiting tribal women knew how to shoot a bow and arrow, the Natayeh women competed against each other, just as they had the last time the two tribes were together. The Zakenaque men and women were amazed at the accuracy of the Natayeh women. Some of the visiting women expressed a desire to learn how to shoot a bow and arrow. The Natayeh women graciously offered to teach these women in private. Keenatay felt that this was definitely a custom that was long overdue for his tribe to embrace.

Now, it was the children's turn to compete with their bow and arrows. Boys from both tribes were matched up according to age to ensure fairness. There were more boys from the Natayeh participating since very few children had made the long trip. The boys from both tribes did surprisingly well. Yukawe won the competition for his age group.

Then, it was the girls' turn. There were seven Natayeh girls carrying bows and arrows. Sartaya went last because she was the oldest girl competing. When it was her turn to shoot, a strange silence fell over the entire crowd. Sabenta made sure she was there to support the girl who had saved her life. Nakia was there, too. Maskanini, Miantra, and Wakishtay watched their granddaughter as well. Almost everyone from both tribes was there. Everyone wanted to see this girl who had saved Sabenta's life by killing a bear with her bow and arrows.

Sartaya sat next to Sabenta, just as she had every day of the games and contests. Before she left to compete, she bent over Sabenta and gently hugged her. "Wish me luck," she said. The woman smiled and nodded. Then, Sartaya walked over to where Nakia was resting on Sabenta's other side. She got down on one knee and patted his head, then whispered, "I love you. I'll be back soon." Nakia licked her hand for good luck.

As Sartaya went to take her first shot, Wakishtay noted her air of complete confidence. He also noticed her reddened arm and knew the spirit of Nakia's mother was with her. As she approached the position for her first target, all the Zakenaque stood up in silence. They all made a fist with their right hand and brought it to their chests, then opened their hand and pointed it toward the girl who saved Sabenta's life. Sartaya wasn't sure exactly what they meant by their gesture, but she thought it was to wish her luck.

She shot every grass target in the highest score colored circle. Many of the other contestants, both boys and girls of all ages, were glad they didn't have to compete against her. When she finished her field of targets, she rejoined Sabenta. "You were wonderful out there today, Sartaya. Your grandparents must be very proud of you." Sartaya blushed as she reached over to pet Nakia.

The smaller targets were removed. Now, only the large, grass animal targets were strategically placed throughout the contest field. It was time for the spear throwing contests. Lakato looked forward to this part of the competition. His tribe was sure he would win any contest that required a spear. However, Keenatay was even more excited to get to this contest. *There will be a lot of very surprised Natayeh contestants when I throw my spear*, he thought. *Let the Great Spirit guide my spears to their intended targets.*

Each tribe put their best spear thrower last in the competition. So Keenatay was paired with Lakato. After all of the other men finished, the results favored the Natayeh. The Natayeh, including Lakato, were sure they would win. Even KiaNeeishtay was confident his people had the edge in this contest.

But after throwing their spears at targets spaced from forty-five to one-hundred five paces away, it was clear the two men were evenly matched. Though Lakato and the rest of the Natayeh were beginning to admire Keenatay's skill with a spear.

At Keenatay's request, four additional large, grass targets were placed on the field. Three were placed at one-hundred, one-hundred eighty, two-hundred ten paces from the two spear throwers. The final one was set down three-hunderd paces away.

Keenatay motioned to Lakato to throw first. As Lakato stepped up to the line to throw his spear at the nearest target, he smiled at his opponent. *I wonder why he asked for these additional targets. They're so far away neither one of us will be able to hit them. It will be good for a few laughs anyway.* Lakato threw his spear with all of his strength. It fell about fifteen paces short of the target. *I feel pretty good about that throw. Now, let's see what Keenatay can do.*

Keenatay stepped up to the throwing line with an air of confidence. With a mischievous smile, he glanced at Lakato.

That's a strange looking spear, Lakato thought, seeing the strange wooden device at the end of Keenatay's spear. *I've never seen anything like it.* With what seemed little effort, Keenatay, threw his spear one-hundred fifty paces, piercing the target in the second highest colored ring. The Zakenaque cheered loudly for their leader. The Natayeh were silent, astonished at what they had just witnessed. Lakato dropped his spear to the ground in surprise and thrust his arms out in front of him, exclaiming, "What? What just happened? I can't believe my eyes!" He turned to his competitor in disbelief.

Keenatay smiled. "Are you ready for the next one?"

"No! It's not possible! No one can throw a spear that far," Lakato said.

Keenatay stepped up to the throwing line for the next target that was one-hundred eighty paces away. He took a deep breath and, with a little more effort than last time, heaved his spear into a higher arc towards the target. Everyone held their breath as the spear took flight. It made a clear thumping noise as it passed through the intended grass figure and stuck in the ground. Everyone, including the Natayeh, cheered loudly.

Keenatay, very proud of himself, strode over to throw his spear at the next target which was two-hundred ten paces away. He stepped up to the throwing line, got into his throwing stance, and released his spear once again. This arc of his spear was even higher than last time. No one spoke while the spear flew through the air. It looked like it was headed directly toward the intended target, but it landed 8 paces past it. Still, it was an incredible effort. Everyone cheered as though he had hit it. Lakato walked over to his opponent and said, "You win. You win. I concede. What you did was amazing. Are you going to go for the last target?"

Keenatay nodded. "I want to show you and your people just how far this device can help you throw a spear. It's called an atlatl—*a spear thrower.*" As he stepped up to the throwing line for the last and farthest target, many people shook their heads, saying it was not possible to throw anything that far. Keenatay positioned himself about eight paces behind the throwing line. He ran to the line, and threw the spear with all his strength. This time the arc was extremely high. The spear seemed to have wings as it flew higher and further, becoming difficult to see. As gravity finally won the battle over height and distance, the spear landed and stuck in the ground beside the grass image of a deer. Even Keenatay was surprised at how close he came to the target. He threw his hands up into to the air in jubilation. Lakato raced over and embraced him enthusiastically.

"You are the best spear thrower I have ever seen." The Zakenaque rushed to congratulate him. Everyone cheered.

The games and the contests were now officially over. KiaNeeishtay couldn't have been happier. *Both our people have a lot to be proud of. Our people have performed well. In a few days, the Zakenaque will leave for their homeland. It's going to be very difficult for Keenatay to leave Sabenta behind,* he guessed. *At least she is alive. And once she's well enough to travel, then what? How will she get back to her home? Who of my tribe will make the long journey with her? I need to discuss this with Maskanini and Miantra.*

After the cheering settled down, Lakato walked over to Keenatay and asked, "Will you show me how to make and use a spear thrower? No one in my tribe has ever seen such a weapon. Where did you learn about it and who taught you how to use it?"

Keenatay smiled. "Of course, that was one of my reasons for this trip. I wanted to share this with your tribe. Two strangers, who visited my tribe four summers ago, taught me how to make and use it. They were from tribes further south and to the west of the Zakenaque. They told me their people have used the spear thrower for many generations. It's helped us kill many elk and deer from further distances than we were used to. I must go to Sabenta's shelter now, but I'll see you later tonight at the campfire."

Lakato nodded and headed for his own shelter. *It must be time for our evening meal. I'm really hungry.* As he got closer to his shelter, he replayed the contest in his mind. *I was so sure I was going to show them how to throw a spear better. I couldn't have been more wrong. I guess there can always be someone better at something than you are.*

Almost everyone from both tribes attended the evening campfire. KiaNeeishtay turned the entire evening of Story Telling over to the Zakenaque. It was their day to brag and brag they did. There was much exaggeration and much laughter among all who gathered around the campfire. It was very, very late by the time the last people headed to their shelters for a well-deserved night's sleep.

CHAPTER 30

Maskanini and Miantra were at Sabenta's shelter tending to her injuries. The wounds still required cleaning and new applications of the medicinal paste. The injured woman's shoulder was healing well and they thought that within several full moons or so, she would have more motion in her arm. In the meantime, they encouraged her to exercise it each day. Her other wounds were also improving. The two caretakers took great pains to keep these wounds clean from infection. This constant care required the two healers to spend most of their time with the injured woman in her shelter.

The same held true for Sartaya and Yukawe who were now the primary caretakers of Nakia. His wounds and ribs healed slowly. "Sartaya, do you think Nakia will ever go hunting with us again? Will he ever be able to run as he once did?"

"His spirit is strong. Otherwise, he never would have survived. It will take awhile, but he'll run and hunt with us again. His mother's spirit has been with him since the attack. I know she's proud of him, just as I am, for saving Sabenta's life. He never once thought about himself."

Sartaya did the same, Yukawe thought. *She didn't think about what could have happened to her. She just shot two arrows into the bear, hoping that would drive it away. I'm so proud of her. I'm honored to be her friend, and Nakia's friend, too.*

Early the next day, KiaNeeishtay stopped by Sabenta's shelter to ask Maskanini and Miantra to join him at his shelter. Wakishtay had also been invited. Miikwasi had prepared a morning meal for all of them at KiaNeeishtay's request. Once everyone arrived, Maskanini asked, "What did you want to discuss with us?"

"Soon, Keenatay and his people will be leaving to journey back to their homeland. Sabenta isn't healthy enough to travel with them. When do you think she'll be strong enough to make that trip, if at all?"

"Maybe around this time late next summer or early fall. Why do you ask?"

"She won't be able to travel alone. I'm thinking several of our people should go with her. What do you all think?"

"The three of us would volunteer but we're too old. Whoever goes should be strong and very good hunters," Wakishtay replied.

"There's also something else to consider," Miantra added. "What if Sabenta or any of her party had an accident and were hurt . . . or one of them gets sick? Who would help them?"

"I've been thinking about that ever since the bear attack. I have some ideas, but before I talk with Keenatay I would like to have a plan," KiaNeeishtay said.

"I can't speak for Lakato, but he, Bosaata, and Yukawe would make good companions for Sabenta and Wanectasii on such a long journey. Lakato is strong and a very good hunter. Yukawe is becoming a good hunter and can track very well. He is also a young man of fifteen summers. You were only twelve summers old when your mother and father took you on the same journey," Wakishtay said.

"I'll speak to them about this. Is there anyone else who could help and might benefit from the experience of such a journey?" The question caught them all by surprise, but there was no mistaking who he meant when he had asked the question.

"Let us think about this," replied Miantra. "If we can think of anyone, we'll let you know." Having said that, she quickly arose and said, "I must get back to Sabenta's shelter. She needs fresh medicine for her wounds." She turned away, hoping none of the men had noticed the fearful tears welling up in her eyes.

The two brothers, meanwhile, gazed at KiaNeeishtay. Wakishtay and his Brother Maskanini, knew this day would eventually come. But, they weren't ready for it to come quite so soon.

But even though she's only thirteen summers old, she's no ordinary child, they thought. *She's already a very capable tracker and hunter. She's proven she can protect herself and others from even the most ferocious predators. She knows how to gather and prepare plants for food. She knows how to prepare and use medicines to help people when they become ill or are injured. Miantra has taught her well. And our ancient ancestors, medicine men and medicine women from the beginning of time, chose to make her a medicine woman. Her destiny is now calling to her.*

Both men suspected KiaNeeishtay had already thought about these things before he had asked that fateful question. They also knew what their answer would have to be. *Sartaya is not ours to keep for ourselves. As her destiny calls for her, we'll have to let her go.*

"We'll discuss this matter further with Miantra," Maskanini said thoughtfully. KiaNeeishtay nodded, understanding full well what he had just asked of them.

"I'll talk with Lakato and his family about making this journey. Give me your answer as soon as you can. I must speak with Keenatay in the next day or so." The leader of the Natayeh arose and headed toward Lakato's shelter.

Miantra knew she must keep herself busy lest her emotions erupt to the surface. As she examined Sabenta's wounds for any sign of infection, Sabenta asked, "What's wrong, Miantra? I can tell something is bothering you. Maybe I can help."

"No, thank you, it's nothing. As soon as I finish, I need to see my granddaughter and check on Nakia. Your wounds are healing very nicely. I know they're still quite painful. Take some more of this medicine when you need it. I'll return later this evening." On her way out of the visitors' campgrounds, she ran into Wanectasii. "Your granddaughter's wounds are healing nicely. I'll come later to check on her again." Then she hurried away before Wanectasii could see how upset she was.

"What is wrong with Miantra?" Wanectasii asked her granddaughter as she entered the shelter. "She had tears in her eyes when I ran into her."

"I wish I knew. She seemed eager to see her granddaughter and to check up on Nakia. I hope he's healing and will be alright."

KiaNeeishtay ran into Lakato and asked if he could speak with both him and his mate, Bosaata. Yukawe was at the practice range repairing some of the grass animals. Lakato invited the leader of the Natayeh into his shelter. "What is it that you want to talk about?"

KiaNeeishtay got right to the point. "Sabenta won't be able to travel with Keenatay and her tribe when they leave in several days. She will remain with us so she can heal. Maskanini thinks she'll be well enough to leave around this time next summer or fall. We can't let her and Wanectasii travel alone. Would you, Bosaata, and Yukawe consider traveling with her and her grandmother, so they arrive safely back to her homeland in the Smokey Mountains?"

The couple was not surprised that Sabenta would not be able to make the journey, but they were caught off guard by KiaNeeishtay's request.

"Who else would be going with us?" Lakato asked.

"I'll ask several of our younger men to go with you. I can't tell you right now how many people will be making this trip. Before I talk with Keenatay, I wanted to talk with both of you first."

"What if Sabenta or one of us becomes ill or gets hurt, who will take care of us?" Bosaata asked. "Maskanini and Miantra are too old to make such a long journey. I don't know anything about medicine or how to use it."

"As soon as I know the answers to these questions, I'll share them with you. Would you consider traveling with her and her grandmother?" KiaNeeishtay asked again.

"We'll discuss this with Yukawe. Will you and Miikwasi join us tomorrow for our evening meal? We'll tell you our decision then," Lakato answered.

Unknown to KiaNeeishtay, Keenatay had met with several of his people to ask them a similar favor. Jakqua, Giniwa, and his mate Sicaasii, had agreed to stay behind until Sabenta could make the long journey back to their homeland. They felt honored to be asked to take on this great responsibility of helping Keenatay's future mate rejoin him the following summer or fall. The two men were skilled hunters and well-respected in their tribe. Sicaasii had all the skills expected of a woman and was well-known for the beautiful clothes she made for herself and her mate. Keenatay was elated these trusted friends would stay behind with the love of his life, and then help her return home.

Now, I need to discuss this matter with KiaNeeishtay, then with Sabenta and her grandmother. I don't want Sabenta worrying about staying behind and becoming a burden to the Natayeh, or how and when she would be rejoining me. Though, I can hardly bear the thought of leaving her behind, he thought. *I'll miss her with all of my heart. I'm thankful to the Great Spirit for sparing her life. By next fall we'll be together and she will be my mate.*

After leaving Sabenta's shelter and running into Wanectasii, Miantra headed directly to her own shelter. *I must compose myself so Sartaya doesn't sense my fear for her. She's too young to travel so far away. She shouldn't be expected to go until our tribe travels there again. This is just wrong. I can't lose her, too.*

Her tears cascaded down her wrinkled and weathered cheeks. She turned away from her shelter and headed for the stream. "Why would KiaNeeishtay even suggest that Sartaya join Lakato, Bosaata, and Yukawe on this journey next summer?" she quietly whispered to herself. "She is just a child!"

As she stood at the water's edge, Maskanini came up behind her and whispered softly, "Miantra. I saw you head toward the stream. I know what's bothering you. Let's sit here for awhile and talk."

"No! I already know what you are going to say and I disagree. She's too young to travel so far. We can't let her go. We just can't!"

"My wonderful mate, how I love your concern for Sartaya. You're a good grandmother. This decision is for both of us to make. Hear what I have to say. Then, if you still feel the same, we'll tell KiaNeeishtay what our decision is."

Miantra reluctantly sat down next to the man she had loved for so long. He placed his arm around her and held her to him gently, but firmly. "Our granddaughter is very special in so many ways. In just a few summers of her life, she has made us very proud. She's also made the Natayeh proud. Everyone loves her. Now, even the Zakenaque admire and love her.

"We've taken care of Sartaya since her birth, but we both know the Great Spirit has also been watching over her and guiding her throughout her life. Just as He has guided the decisions we have made in our lives, He's influenced Sartaya's choices and experiences throughout these past thirteen summers of her life. We both know in our hearts that the Great Spirit has a very special destiny for our granddaughter. He's protected her, but at the same time has exposed her to experiences that no other has had. Our tribe's very existence may depend upon her someday.

"Recently, the Great Spirit instructed our ancient ancestral medicine men and medicine women to make Sartaya a medicine woman, filling her spirit with all their combined knowledge. I know we've asked ourselves this question before, but we must ask ourselves again. 'Why has our granddaughter had all of these challenging experiences at such a young age?' There's only one answer to this question. The Great Spirit needed her to have them. He, who knows all, knew she had to live these experiences when she did."

Maskanini paused pulling Miantra even closer to him. "Only the Great Spirit knows these things. Her age doesn't matter to He who knows all. It only matters to you and me. He'll protect her and guide her long after we've joined our ancestors in the sky. If the Great Spirit wants her to go on this journey, He has prepared her well. Even though her age is that of a child, her spirit is that of a woman, a medicine woman. Think about what I have said tonight. Ask your spirit to help you with your decision. In the morning, we'll make a decision together. Come, I'll walk with you back to our shelter."

"Grandmother, you've been crying," Sartaya exclaimed when Miantra and her grandfather entered their shelter.

"It's something in the air, Sartaya. How is Nakia? Has he been standing and walking around?"

"Yes, Grandmother, Yukawe's been helping me lift Nakia to his feet. Then, he encourages Nakia to walk towards him with meat in his hands. I think Nakia knows the routine now and is playing a game with us. Yukawe went home for his evening meal. He promised to come back to help me tomorrow morning. He's been a lot of help."

"Why don't you and your grandfather go for a walk? It'll be

awhile before the evening meal is ready. Nakia will keep me company."

"Grandfather, why is Grandmother sad?" Sartaya asked as they strolled to the edge of the campsite.

"We all become sad from time to time. Sometimes, we can share our sadness and other times we can't. If she chooses not to share her feelings with you or me, it doesn't mean she loves us any less. Sometimes, we keep our feelings to ourselves because we don't want to burden others with them. Now, where would you like to walk?"

"How is Sabenta doing?" Sartaya asked. "Will she be staying with us until she's better? She's going to feel very alone when the rest of her tribe leaves. Will her grandmother remain behind, too? How can we make her and her grandmother feel more at home here?"

"Sartaya, you have so many questions. Sabenta is healing slowly, but that's good. She will be lonesome, especially for Keenatay. Why don't you think about some of the ways we all can help her and her grandmother feel more at home while they stay here with us?"

By the time their evening meal was over, the last rays of sunlight were fading in the western sky. Maskanini and Miantra visited Sabenta to check and treat her wounds. When they finished they left for their own shelter.

CHAPTER 31

Miantra was tired, but she couldn't fall asleep. Her mind whirled with thoughts of Sartaya on a journey to the Smokey Mountains. Finally, well into the night, she fell into a deep sleep. In a dream she was awakened by loud voices. While trying to see where these voices came from, she was suddenly surrounded by many of her ancient ancestors. Not all of them were medicine men and medicine women, but she recognized everyone. They all faced her and talked at the same time.

"Miantra, you must let Sartaya go. We made her a medicine woman so she could care for Nakia while you and Maskanini cared for Sabenta. She must help Sabenta become a medicine woman. The Zakenaque do not have a Maskanini or medicine woman. The Great Spirit wishes for Sabenta to become the medicine woman for their tribe. Sartaya must go with her and Nakia must also go with them."

Several times throughout the night Miantra's spirit shouted out her disagreements. On several occasions, her outbursts flowed over into her physical self and startled everyone else in the shelter. Maskanini and Sartaya wisely kept to themselves and did their best to fall back to sleep, only to be awakened again by another outburst.

"Miantra, you're only thinking with your heart and about yourself. There are things far greater than your own discomforts and fears," thundered the Great Spirit. "Sartaya is the future of the Natayeh, but she must first make this journey with Sabenta. Sabenta will be the future of the Zakenaque. Their experiences, together on this journey, will make them stronger so they can both fulfill their destinies. Now sleep, and when you awaken in the morning, you'll know the decision that you must make." While she slept, Maskanini and Sartaya lay awake, each having been roused one too many times by the old woman's outbursts. Maskanini could guess what was making his mate so angry. Sartaya, however, didn't have any idea about what was bothering her grandmother until she too was visited that night by some of her ancient ancestors.

As the morning sunlight prodded the two tribes awake, Miantra awoke feeling unusually at ease. What the Great Spirit had told her put her at peace with herself and the decision she had come to. As Maskanini stirred, he met the gaze of his longtime mate. He knew immediately that she had come to the same decision he had with regards to Sartaya traveling with Sabenta. He smiled at her lovingly.

After their morning meal they both headed over to KiaNeeishtay's shelter. He spotted them as he was finishing his hot morning drink.

"KiaNeeishtay, we've made our decision. Sartaya will go with Sabenta next fall," Maskanini said.

"I'm grateful to you both. Have you spoken to your granddaughter about this?"

"No. We'll speak to her later this morning," Miantra offered. Having said that, Sartaya's grandparents left KiaNeeishtay and headed back to their shelter.

KiaNeeishtay still had two men of his tribe he needed to speak with about joining Sabenta on her journey back to her homeland. *That must have been a very difficult decision for them both to make, especially for Miantra. She lives for that little girl. I wonder how Sartaya will take to the idea of such a long trip without her grandmother.*

KiaNeeishtay met up with the two men he would entrust with the lives and safety of Sabenta and Sartaya. Enostabi and Shuntundia agreed without hesitation to make the journey. They felt deeply honored their tribal leader had offered them this great responsibility. Both men had come to know and love Sartaya. And they both had made this trip as boys when KiaNeeishtay's father and mother had taken him with them to visit the Zakenaque.

Now I must meet with Keenatay to share my plan for Sabenta's safe return next fall. He would do the same for me or anyone else in the Natayeh, thought KiaNeeishtay. He felt very satisfied with his plan, one he was sure that Keenatay would approve.

Later that day, the Natayeh leader met with Keenatay. "Welcome to my campfire, KiaNeeishtay. Sit here next to me," he said.

KiaNeeishtay nodded and sat down beside his new friend. KiaNeeishtay said, "As you know, Sabenta won't be able to return with you when you leave in several days. I've made arrangements to have a shelter built for her and her grandmother next to Maskanini's shelter. Sabenta will be safe and cared for by Maskanini and Miantra during her stay, especially during the winter season. I've also asked several of my most trusted people to travel with Sabenta next fall when she should be healed enough to return home. Sartaya's grandparents have agreed to allow their granddaughter to also make the journey. Lakato, his mate, Bosaata, and his son, Yukawe have also agreed to travel. Two of my best men, Enostabi and Shuntundia, said they would be honored to travel with Sabenta. They've both been to the Zakenaque village before. Will you consider these arrangements and let me know if they'll be alright with you, Sabenta, and Wanectasii?"

Keenatay was speechless. He looked directly into the eyes of the Natayeh leader. "You are truly my brother. You have thought of everything. I, too, have asked several of my most trusted people if they would remain behind and travel with Sabenta next fall. Jakqua, Giniwa and his mate, Sicaasii, have agreed to stay behind. I felt it was too much for me to ask you if some of your people would consider traveling with Sabenta next fall. You've lifted a great burden from my shoulders. Thank you." The two tribal leaders clasped each other's right forearms. The stained colors on each of their right arms, although faded somewhat, formed a circle once again.

"We'll help Jakqua, Giniwa and Sicaasii build their shelters within our main campgrounds. Don't worry. They'll be our honored guests for as long as they're here." Keenatay nodded his appreciation.

"Tomorrow we'll have a special evening meal for both tribes," said KiaNeeishtay. "We'll celebrate the friendship between our people. Then, after the meal, we'll have a special campfire to honor all of your people and to ask the Great Spirit to help you on your journey back to your homeland. The women from both our tribes have already been planning for the food. I know you've been spending a lot of time with Sabenta. How is she?"

"She is healing slowly. Both Maskanini and Miantra assure me this is the way her wounds are supposed to heal," Keenatay answered. "She's in constant pain, but she very rarely shows it. When I dress her wounds, instead of squinting in pain she smiles and touches my hand. I love this woman with all my heart and spirit. I can hardly bear the thought of leaving her behind. But after talking with you, I know she'll be rejoining me next fall. This brings much peace to my mind. Thank you, again. Will you ask Maskanini and Miantra to bring Sartaya and Nakia with them to the campfire tomorrow evening? I want to honor them for saving Sabenta's life. Sabenta and her grandmother will also be there."

KiaNeeishtay nodded. "I'll see to it. I am also glad Sabenta and her grandmother will be able to attend. Will you sit by my side at the campfire?"

"I will be honored to sit next to you," replied Keenatay. "Thank you again, my brother, for what you have done to ease my mind about Sabenta. I'll see you tonight. Right now, I have to help my people prepare for the journey back to our homeland." Both men smiled at each other before they parted.

"Sartaya, your grandfather and I want to discuss something with you," Miantra said as she and Maskanini entered their shelter.

"What is it, Grandmother? Does it have something to do with what's been bothering you?" "Yes, Granddaughter, it does. Sabenta will be staying behind when Keenatay and the others leave to return home. We believe she'll be well enough to make the trip by next fall. Lakato, Bosaata, and Yukawe will be going with her. Others will be going as well, I'm sure.

"We can't be sure of her needs on this long trip. Most of her injuries should be healed by then. But if she or any of the others get hurt or become ill, they'll need someone who can help them. Grandfather and I are too old to make this trip. He and I think you should go with her." Miantra paused to let Sartaya absorb everything she had just said. The girl's face showed little surprise, almost as if she had expected this conversation.

"Grandmother, I've known for awhile Sabenta would remain behind with her grandmother. The ancients have been visiting me in my dreams since that day you and I were told I was to be a medicine woman. They've shown me things that haven't happened, yet I'm to be a part of. When they showed me traveling with Sabenta next fall, I told them I couldn't go without your approval. Then, last night when I finally fell asleep, they told me they had visited you. They told me you both would talk with me sometime in the morning."

Maskanini and Miantra were surprised by this revelation. "What else have the ancients been telling you, Sartaya?" Maskanini asked curiously.

"They said the Zakenaque no longer had a medicine man and they had decided to make Sabenta a medicine woman. They told me they wanted me to teach her everything you've taught me, as well as what they've shared with me. Between now and when she arrives back home, they want me to care for her wounds and teach her what I know about medicine and healing. They also said Nakia would be fully healed by next summer and would be able to travel with us. I was so relieved to hear that."

"The Great Spirit works in mysterious ways. Maskanini and I are happy for you and very proud of you. We'll miss you greatly, but we know you'll be returning to us by the beginning of next winter or, at the latest, the following summer. We know we can't keep you for ourselves, that we must share you with others. Did you already know that Lakato, Bosaata, and Yukawe were going on this journey with you?"

"No, I couldn't see any of the faces of those traveling with us. But I did see that there were twelve of us including Nakia. I'm happy Yukawe and his family will be going with us. He's my closest friend."

Miantra smiled. *So, the Great Spirit does keep some surprises to Himself.* "We have the coming seasons to share with you before you leave. We'll make the most of that time." They all nodded and smiled affectionately at each other.

Sartaya embraced her grandmother and grandfather. "Thank you for loving me so much. My heart will ache from missing you both while I'm away. I'll look forward with great joy to the day I return home to you." They all had tears of sadness and joy running freely down their cheeks.

CHAPTER 32

Word spread quickly throughout both tribes that there was going to be a feast and ceremonial campfire the next evening. All were expected to attend, including Nakia. By now, the entire Zakenaque had adopted the wolf as their brother. They all prayed to the Great Spirit for his quick and complete recovery. They would see to it that their adopted brother had some choice meat at tomorrow's feast. Both tribes spent much of the day preparing for the following evening's events. When all the preparations were completed, the members of both tribes relaxed into their evening routines and eventually closed their eyes to end another day.

Excitement stirred in both camps the next day as everyone anticipated the upcoming events. Keenatay was cleaning Sabenta's wounds when she grabbed his right hand and held it firmly to her heart. She looked directly into his eyes and smiled. "Don't worry about leaving me behind. I'll be well taken care of. Maskanini and Miantra have both told me I will be healed enough by late next summer to make the journey back to our homeland . . . and to you. I believe them," she said.

"I'll miss you terribly," she continued, "but I know in my heart and spirit we'll be together again and grow old in each other's arms. This, the Great Spirit has promised me. Also, don't worry about not having a Maskanini in our tribe. The Great Spirit and many of our ancient ancestors visited me while I was in a death sleep after the attack. They asked me if I would become the medicine woman for our tribe. I told them I would. Then, I had a vision of Sartaya teaching me to be a medicine woman."

"I'll miss you also. But, after KiaNeeishtay's visit, I feel better about having to leave you behind," Keenatay said. He told Sabenta everything he and the Natayeh leader had discussed the day before.

"I asked KiaNeeishtay to make sure Sartaya, Nakia, and her grandparents attended the ceremonial campfire tonight so we can honor them. He promised he would." Then Keenatay finished cleansing her wounds and refreshing the medicinal paste used on them. After he pulled her garment back up to her shoulders and tied the straps that held it together, he gently raised her up and kissed her lovingly. It hurt as he embraced her, but that was a small price to pay for the joy she felt being held in his strong but gentle arms.

CHAPTER 33

Everyone from both tribes enjoyed the feast prepared by the Natayeh and Zakenaque women. Nakia was especially happy when several men from the Zakenaque stopped by to drop off some generous servings of prime deer meat for him. He allowed them to touch his head and ears while they told him how brave he was. He no longer smelled their fear, but instead, sensed their love and respect for him. Keenatay, Sabenta, and Wanectasii joined KiaNeeishtay and Miikwasi for the feast. Sabenta took this opportunity to tell KiaNeeishtay how much she appreciated his invitation to stay with his tribe until she got better.

"Thank you, KiaNeeishtay, for all that you and your wonderful people have done for me. Although I would like nothing more than to leave with Keenatay and our people, I'm looking forward to my extended visit with the Natayeh." Miikwasi smiled at her mate with pride in her eyes. KiaNeeishtay's face reddened, as he flushed with pride not only for himself, but for his entire tribe.

After everyone had their fill, the women quickly gathered up what food remained and stored it away. When they returned, everyone walked over to the main campfire, which by now was roaring. They seated themselves around the fire ring, each tribe interspersed with the other. Both Sabenta and Nakia walked together, though slowly, over to where the people were gathering. KiaNeeishtay and Miikwasi, Wakishtay, Maskanini and Miantra, Sartaya, Wanectasii, and Keenatay walked behind them. No one was in a hurry. When they arrived at the outside of the fire ring, KiaNeeishtay invited Keenatay, Sabenta, and Wanectasii to sit to his right. His mate, Miikwasi and his mother, Kyashee, had already seated themselves far to his right, allowing plenty of room for the three visitors to sit. Sartaya, Nakia, Maskanini, Miantra, and Wakishtay sat to the leader's left.

Once everyone was seated, KiaNeeishtay stood. Silence enveloped the entire gathering. "It seems like just yesterday that the Zakenaque arrived at the Natayeh campsite. Now, our visitors are preparing to start their long journey back to their homeland. The Natayeh would like to thank you for traveling so far to visit with us. We are honored to have you as our guests. At one of our many campfires together, I told you the story of how this mountain lion, whose head is on a pole behind me, attacked Sartaya and Yukawe and how it was then killed by these same brave children. At a ceremony, shortly after the mountain lion was killed, we gave each and every member of the Natayeh a piece of bone from this lion. Tonight, we would like to give each of you a piece of bone from this mountain lion." He nodded to Sartaya, Yukawe, and Maskanini. The two children each had a bowl filled with pieces of the mountain lion's bones. They stood up in front of Maskanini. He took the two bowls and raised them to the star-filled evening sky.

"I call upon Chanutey, the mountain lion's spirit, to join us tonight. Our visitors have a long and challenging journey ahead of them. We are giving each of them a piece of your strong bones and ask that your spirit provide them with the strength to meet their challenges and get home safely." Maskanini gave the two bowls back to Yukawe and Sartaya. They went around to each visitor and let them pick out a piece of the mountain lion's bones. When they had finished, they returned to their seats.

Once again, the leader of the Natayeh stood up and silence followed. He nodded to Keenatay, who stood up to speak. He looked to the evening sky and called upon their ancestors who sparkled above them. "Soon we will be making the long journey back to our homeland. Thanks to the people of the Natayeh we now have Chanutey's bones to fill our spirits with courage and help us on our journey home."

He turned and looked at Sabenta affectionately. "Many wonderful things have happened while we have visited. But a vicious bear attack, which almost took the lives of Sabenta and Nakia, will be what most of us remember from our visit here. I want to help change that memory. I want everyone to remember the raw courage that it took for Sartaya and Nakia to drive the fierce bear away from Sabenta . . . saving her life. I want everyone to remember the price that Nakia paid when he tried to save the woman that I love.

"I want everyone to remember the dedication that Maskanini and Miantra showed in saving Sabenta's life and caring for her. Her wounds were so severe that she entered our ancestors' dominion, even talked with their spirits, and then returned to us. If not for Maskanini and Miantra, she most likely would not be here with us tonight. There were many nights they did not get any rest at all. But, they never gave up on her. I will never forget what they have done for Sabenta, for me, and for all of us.

"I want you to remember the generous people of the Natayeh who brought food and water to Sabenta's shelter each and every day. No one asked them for their help, but they did it anyways. Their thoughtfulness filled the bellies of Maskanini, Miantra, Wanectasii, and me. They not only did that for us, but each day they also provided food to Sartaya and Wakishtay who were caring for Nakia, while her grandparents took care of Sabenta.

"The Natayeh are very special people. I consider KiaNeeishtay, leader of the Natayeh, to be my brother. I would give my life for him." He paused and turned once again to Sabenta. She nodded. "Sabenta would like to honor those who have saved her life and who have cared for her all this time. She cannot talk loud enough for all of you to hear, so I will speak her words for her. 'I am grateful to all of you who have given me back my life. I promise each and every one of you that I will honor this gift of life by helping others in every possible way. The bear attack was horrible, but I do not blame the bear for what he did to me and to Nakia. He was just being what Mother Earth created him to be, a bear. While I slept deeply for days at a time, the bear's spirit came to me. At first, I didn't understand what he was trying to tell me. Then my spirit explained to me what he was saying. The bear's spirit was sorry for attacking us. He asked the Great Spirit if he could now watch over and protect us from harm. The Great Spirit agreed. I asked Keenatay to take the bear's claws and make a necklace with one bear claw for each of you who have cared for me.' "

She handed Keenatay the necklaces and asked him to give them to Sartaya, Nakia, Maskanini, Miantra, and Wanectasii. Then, she asked the man whom she loved more than anything else to bend over toward her. When he did, she placed a necklace over his head. Keenatay smiled affectionately and thanked her.

He then looked over to Maskanini and nodded. Maskanini stood and raised both hands to the evening sky. His hands clutched a beautiful necklace made up of the remaining bear claws interspersed with small opaque shells. Directing his words to the twinkling lights high above them, Maskanini said, "I call upon all of the ancestors of both the Zakenaque and the Natayeh who have gathered in the night sky above us. You have all witnessed the attack on Sabenta by a fierce black bear. The black bear is the largest and strongest animal in our forests. Yet, Sabenta survived this ferocious animal's attack and its spirit is now up there with you. We will call it Kahutey and the claws in this necklace will remind everyone of Kahutey's great strength. That strength now belongs to Sabenta. The spirit of the bear will now protect her and all who wear one of its claws." Maskanini handed the necklace to Keenatay who placed it carefully around Sabenta's neck. She smiled gratefully at the man who would someday be her mate. Everyone stood and cheered loudly.

Keenatay then turned to KiaNeeishtay who smiled and nodded his approval. "I could not leave for my homeland without honoring a very special member of the Natayeh. This person has shown great courage. This person has the hunting skills of the very best of hunters. This person has a heart as big as the moon and one that shines brighter than the sun. This person, without any regard for her own safety, killed a fierce bear with two of her arrows, saving the life of the woman I love. Sartaya, will you please stand?"

Sartaya's cheeks were red from embarrassment. KiaNeeishtay encouraged her to stand up. As she did, all the Zakenaque stood and cheered as they clinched their right hand into a fist and brought it to their chests. Then they opened their clenched hands and pointed them directly at Sartaya, cheering more loudly than before. Sartaya didn't know what to think. This is what they had done when she stood up to shoot at the competition games.

"Sartaya, this gesture by my people is the highest honor we can give to someone. It means we are of one heart with your heart, forever." Keenatay motioned to several of his people. They immediately unfolded a huge bear skin and held it up in front of her. "This is yours, Sartaya. I hope it brings you much comfort in the coming winter season. Sabenta said Kahutey wanted you to have it." Sartaya shrieked with excitement and surprise as she reached to touch the beautifully finished soft hide. The two men then folded the large bearskin and placed it on the ground in front of her. All the members from both tribes stood and cheered for the girl who had shown such great courage in killing the fierce bear and saving the life of Sabenta.

KiaNeeishtay signaled that the ceremonial campfire was over. But it was well into the night before most left the main campfire for their own shelters. It seemed as though no one wanted the night to end.

Wakishtay carried the bear skin for Sartaya while Maskanini and Miantra walked with her and Nakia back to their shelter. They all marveled at how soft and beautiful the bear skin was. Sartaya asked her grandfather to place the folded skin in the back of their shelter until she could decide what to do with it. She embraced Wakishtay and thanked him for carrying the skin. He left for his own shelter, feeling light-hearted after the embrace with his granddaughter. Nakia was tired and feeling the pain from his wounds after being up and about for so long. He just wanted to lie down and close his eyes. Sartaya embraced her grandparents and wished them both a good night's rest. She then lay down next to Nakia on the soft warm hide of his mother and fell quickly into a deep sleep. Maskanini and Miantra fell asleep soon afterwards.

Many members from both tribes slept late into the next morning. The visiting tribe decided to leave the following day for their homeland. The Natayeh promised they would serve them a morning meal and then help them pack their shelters for travel. The thought of returning home filled the hearts of the visitors with joyful anticipation, while the thought of everything returning to normal filled the hearts of the Natayeh. Work had already begun on the new shelter for Sabenta and Wanectasii. Many Natayeh men had already promised Jakqua, Giniwa and Sicaasii they would help them build more permanent shelters.

Keenatay spent as much of the day as he could spare with Sabenta. She surprised Keenatay with a parting gift she and her grandmother had made for him. When he unfolded the small hide, it revealed an extraordinary dream catcher.

"It's beautiful, Sabenta," he exclaimed. The look in his eyes and smile on his face were all the thanks she needed. He embraced her one last time, wishing he never had to let her go. "I will keep this close to me always," he whispered.

After he left Sabenta, Keenatay wiped the moisture from his eyes and made his way over to KiaNeeishtay's shelter. The two men spoke privately for a short while. Only their spirits know what they discussed. Afterwards, they faced each other and clasped their right forearms to complete the stained half circles.

Other tribal members from each camp also took advantage of the day to say their goodbyes to one another, many exchanging small mementos. Keenatay also made one last visit to Maskanini's shelter. There, he once again expressed his heartfelt gratitude to Maskanini, Miantra, Sartaya, and Nakia for all that they had done for Sabenta.

"Sartaya, I'm already looking forward to seeing you again soon." He didn't see Miantra wince from the thought of her granddaughter traveling so far away without her. "I understand Sabenta will be spending much time with the three of you, learning about medicines. It makes me happy to know she will be surrounded by people who care so deeply for her." He knelt down next to Nakia and gently stroked the wolf's head. "I hope I'll see you, too, when I see your sister, next fall." Nakia responded by licking the leader's hand.

Following a morning meal that the Natayeh prepared for them, the Zakenaque packed up their belongings with the help of their host tribe. It was mid-morning by the time they made their way around the Natayeh campsite and waved goodbye to their new-found friends and brothers. This time, though, Nakia and Sartaya were positioned directly in their path, as Keenatay had requested. Every member of the Zakenaque said goodbye to both of them with their special gesture of hand to heart. A few of their tribal men dropped off choice pieces of raw meat in front of Nakia, which he greatly appreciated as he immediately consumed them.

Sabenta and Wanectasii were positioned just a little further up on the path of the travelers. Every member of their tribe wished them well as they said goodbye. Keenatay knelt beside Sabenta. He wrapped his powerful arms around her frail body and hugged her tightly. He whispered "Come back to me soon."

She whispered. "I, too, will miss you. I promise you we will be together before next winter. I will send all of my dreams to your dream catcher. Keep it close to you always." Keenatay nodded as he fingered the dream catcher hanging from his neck and resting over his heart.

He then caught up to the rest of his tribe. He paused for a moment to steal one last look at the Natayeh people who had made such a deep and lasting impression on him and his tribe. As he caught one last glimpse of Sartaya and Nakia, he closed his fist and brought it to his chest and then opened his hand while pointing it directly at them. He then disappeared from sight along with the rest of his people as they descended a small hill to begin their long journey back to the Zakenaque homeland.

EPILOGUE

Sabenta now knew her destiny as clearly as if she had written it herself. She looked forward to being able to help her people in ways she could not have imagined before her visit to the Natayeh.

Sartaya was just beginning to imagine what her destiny held in store for her. Her role as a medicine woman continued to unfold as her ancient ancestors continued to share their secrets of medicine and visions of events yet to take place. Her visions of the future always included Nakia by her side, so she felt confident that he would soon heal completely from his wounds.

Next summer Sartaya would exchange her Necklace of Age for a Life Necklace of her own choosing. She would be fourteen summers old and considered a young woman by the time she began her journey with Sabenta to the Zakenaque village.

Yukawe would be sixteen summers old when he, his mother, and his father join Sabenta on the long journey back to her homeland. His tribe already considered him a young man in search of his own destiny. The friendship between Yukawe and Sartaya would grow stronger with each new summer.

READER'S GUIDE

CHARACTER NAMES, PRONUNCIATIONS MEANINGS & RELATIONSHIPS

Bosaata [Bo sa ta] (Butterfly): Lakato's Mate & Mother to Yukawe

Chanutey [Cha nu tay] (Mountain Lion Spirit): Attacked Sartaya & Yukawe

Chikowa [Chi kow a] (Bear Paw): Miantra's First Mate (Died), Father to Nonca's Mother

Dyoshat [Dy o shot] (Chaser of Fire Flies): One of the boys who set the snare trap

Ebisconni [E bis con ne] (Sparkling Water): Lake where Sartaya's first kill took place.

Enostabi [E nos ta be] (Black Fox): Chosen by KiaNeeishtay to accompany Sabenta back to her homeland

Fenwati [Fen wat e] (Turtle Catcher): One of the boys who set the snare trap

Giniwa [Gin e wa] (Eagle Feather): Sicaasii's Mate & chosen by Keenatay to accompany Sabenta back to her homeland

Jakqua [Ja qua] (Red Hawk): Chosen by Keenatay to accompany Sabenta back to her homeland

Kahutey [Ka hu tay] (Black Bear Spirit): Attacked Sabenta & Nakia

Keenatay [Keen a tay] (Elk Hunter): Zakenaque Tribal Leader

KiaNatay [Kea Na tay] (Chief Gray Wolf): Previous Tribal Chief (Died), Kyashee's Mate, & Father to KiaNeeishtay

KiaNeeishtay [Kea Nee ish tay] (Chief Tracking Wolf): Current Tribal Chief, Son to KiaNatay & Kyashee, & Mate to Miikwasi

Kyashee [Ky a shee] (Bright Star): KiaNatay's Mate & Mother to KiaNeeishtay

Lakato [La kay toe] (Spear Maker): Bosaata's Mate & Father to Yukawe

Maskanini [Mas ka nini] (Tribal Medicine Man): Miantra's Second Mate, Step-Grandfather to Sartaya, & Brother to Wakishtay

Miantra [Me an tra] (Spirit Talker): Was mated to Chikowa (Died), now Maskanini's Mate, Maternal Grandmother to Sartaya, Medicine Woman

Miikwasi [Me ik wa se] (Dream Keeper): KiaNeeishtay's Mate

Nakia [Na ke a] (Wolf Brother): Sartaya's Wolf Brother

Natayeh [Na tay a] (Gray Wolf Tribe): The Gray Wolf Tribe were some of the earliest people to inhabit the North American region some 6,100 summers ago. Their hunting grounds included vast natural resources of forests, rivers, lakes, and streams.

Nonca [Non ca] (Squirrel Chaser): First given name, then changed to Sartaya

Sabenta [Sa ben ta] (Morning Sun): Zakenaque Tribal Woman attacked by Kahutey, Future mate of Keenatay

Sartaya [Sar tay a] (Wolf Sister): Granddaughter to Wakishtay, Miantra, & Maskanini, Sister to Nakia

Shuntundia [Shun tune de a] (Thunder Cloud): Chosen by KiaNeeishtay to accompany Sabenta back to her homeland

Sicaasii [Se ca see] (Cloud Chaser): Giniwa's Mate & chosen by Keenatay to accompany Sabenta back to her homeland

Waawaatesi [Wa wa te se] (Fire Fly): Wakishtay's Mate & Paternal Grandmother to Sartaya (Died)

Wakishtay [Wa kish tay] (Hunting Wolf): Paternal Grandfather to Sartaya, Waawaatesi's Mate & Brother to Maskanini

Wanastabi [Wan a sta be] (Walking Stick): First Keeper of Sacred Walking Stick for Wijomine Tribe

Wanectasii [Wa nec ta se] (Yellow Flower): Sabenta's Grandmother

Wijomine [Wi jo mine] (First People Tribe): Described in Miantra's explanation of Walking Stick Dream

Yukawe [Yu ka way] (Swift Runner): Son to Lakato & Bosaata

Zakenaque [Zak en a que] (Smokey Mountain Tribe): Visiting guest tribe of the Natayeh

Don, the author of Sartaya, enjoys reading almost as much as he enjoys writing. He has always been a storyteller much to the delight of his two sons as they were growing up and then later to the delight of his granddaughters. He lives in Huron, Ohio with his wonderful wife Karen of 48 years.

www.ingramcontent.com/pod-product-compliance
Lightning Source LLC
Chambersburg PA
CBHW061543250926
52052CB00010B/3051
* 9 7 8 1 9 4 0 4 6 6 1 1 8 *